Eli sucke ed
to toy wit it
would aff

Her innocence was obvious, and he knew she hailed from a staunch Christian family; so when he assumed her naive in the ways of a man and a woman, he'd been right. Her kiss was shy and uncertain. This girl wasn't worldly wise. The stunned expression etched on her face at the end of the kiss spoke volumes, and she couldn't get out of his arms fast enough.

What shocked him was his own response. He'd enjoyed holding her, but even more startling, he had the urge to hold her forever—and he wasn't a forever kind of guy. He shook his head to rid himself of the thought. *Delanie Cooper, I won't let you get to me.*

When she returned, he stood and pulled out the wooden chair with the padded seat. "You okay?"

"Fine." Her answer was short and clipped—her cheeks still flushed.

He took the chair to Delanie's right. Fairly certain their kiss had affected her even more than it had him, he decided he'd play it up and kiss her at every opportunity. Maybe then she'd ditch him and this job, and he could go back to his old unit, far away from her and those wide aquamarine eyes.

Taking her hand in his, he leaned over, kissed her cheek, and whispered in her ear, "Remember what Sarge said about being 100 percent believable as a young couple in love?"

Delanie nodded but remained tense. He smiled. His plan was working already.

JERI ODELL is a native of Tucson, Arizona. She has been married almost thirty-five years and is the mother of three wonderful adult children. Two are married, and her first grandbaby is due this month. Jeri holds family dear to her heart, second only to God. She thanks God for the privilege of writing for Him. When not writing or reading, she is busy in her church and community. If you'd like, you can e-mail her at jeriodell@juno.com.

Books by Jeri Odell

HEARTSONG PRESENTS
HP413—Remnant of Victory
HP467—Hidden Treasures
HP525—Game of Pretend
HP595—Surrendered Heart

Don't miss out on any of our super romances. Write to us at the following address for information on our newest releases and club information.

Heartsong Presents Readers' Service
PO Box 721
Uhrichsville, OH 44683

Or visit www.heartsongpresents.com

Always Yesterday

Jeri Odell

Heartsong Presents

This book is dedicated to Camden, my first grandson. I have waited a very long time for you, and love you more than you can even imagine. I cannot wait to hold you close, pray over you, and share sweet stories about Jesus. This grandma couldn't be more thrilled. Many thanks to Marti, my cousin, for her medical expertise, to Adam, my son, for his legal expertise, and to Kelsy, my daughter, and Crit goup 11 for their editorial guidance. And last, but not least, the Reno police department for their valuable information about the inner workings of the department. If there is any glory to be had, may it go to my Lord and Savior, Jesus Christ.

A note from the Author:
I love to hear from my readers! You may correspond with me by writing:

Jeri Odell
Author Relations
PO Box 721
Uhrichsville, OH 44683

ISBN 978-1-59789-868-3

ALWAYS YESTERDAY

All scripture quotations, unless otherwise indicated, are taken from the HOLY BIBLE, NEW INTERNATIONAL VERSION®. NIV®. Copyright © 1973, 1978, 1984 by International Bible Society. Used by permission of Zondervan. All rights reserved.

All of the characters and events in this book are fictitious. Any resemblance to actual persons, living or dead, or to actual events is purely coincidental.

Our mission is to publish and distribute inspirational products offering exceptional value and biblical encouragement to the masses.

PRINTED IN THE U.S.A.

one

A searing pain tore through Eli Logan's left shoulder. Warm blood trailed down his chest. Woozy, he grabbed for something—anything—to hold on to. Stumbling toward the warehouse wall, he leaned against it for support. He searched for any sign of his assailant but only caught sight of his partner's pale face and terror-filled eyes. Bernadette had frozen when he needed her most.

The throbbing in his shoulder increased with each erratic breath. Eli holstered his gun and placed his right hand over the bullet wound, feeling a soggy shirt beneath his fingers. "Call for an ambulance!" he yelled at his middle-aged partner, who still hadn't moved. The growing red stain soaking his shirt meant he was losing blood at a quick pace. His knees gave way, and a black fog fought to overpower him. He slid down the wall and hit the ground with a thud. "Dear God, help me."

Eli jerked to a sitting position, sweat drenching him. He touched his left shoulder, expecting blood but finding only a three-month-old scar. Would this nightmare never stop? Untangling himself from the sheets, he headed for the kitchen and a cold drink of water. When would he ever get a full night's sleep again?

His hand trembled when he took the glass from the cupboard. Outside the window a full moon shone overhead, illuminating a cloudless Nevada sky. He filled his glass and let the cool liquid slide down his parched throat. Inhaling deeply, he attempted to slow his pounding heart and calm his breathing.

The clock mocked him. Five minutes after three. Maybe he could still catch a few more hours of shut-eye. Of course, he doubted he'd accomplish that feat. Once the nightmare awoke him, the adrenaline surging through his body guaranteed his day started now.

Lying back down, he stared at the ceiling. Was he ready for tomorrow—his first day back at work since the shooting? He'd undergone surgery, physical therapy, and counseling. All of the professionals said he was good to go, but he remained unconvinced, though he'd never verbalized his doubts. *No, I can do this. I will do this!*

"At least I won't have a woman partner anymore." He mumbled the fact aloud to reassure himself. "Some guy named Delaney." That news brought relief. Women were pleasant to look at, maybe even fun to date once in a while, but they didn't belong on the force. Nor did they belong in his life. He just wished he wasn't so attracted to the pretty ones.

There were three women in his life he'd counted on, and none of them came through when he needed them most. When he was twelve, his mother taught him his first hard lesson about the fairer sex. She packed up and left the day after his sixteen-year-old brother's funeral. Ronny died of a drug overdose. She said she wasn't hanging around to watch Eli do the same. He'd lost both his mother and his brother in a week, and God had done nothing to intervene. So for almost two decades it had been just him and his old man, and his dad had spent most of those eighteen years in a drunken stupor. But he was all the family Eli had, and he loved his dad, tried to watch out for him—at least as much as his dad allowed.

Eli turned his pillow over and punched it, longing to

forget, longing to sleep, but the memories kept coming. Amy—his one and only love, or so he thought—taught him lesson number two. She didn't want him; she wanted his best friend. When he caught them together, he walked away from the pair and never looked back, but he never recovered either. By seventeen he'd learned three hard truths: you can't count on God, you can't count on family, and you can't count on friends.

And let's not forget Bernadette. Good ol' Bernie. She'd grown tired of the traffic scene and wanted more excitement. Well, she'd gotten her wish—only she couldn't handle the thrill. Now that she was restricted to a desk job at the precinct, cruising around writing tickets probably didn't seem so boring to her anymore.

❧

"Sarge, I'm here." Eli rounded the corner into the sergeant's office a few hours later, but his chair sat empty. A movement by the window caught Eli's attention, and there stood one fine-looking woman. His breath caught in his throat, and had he not been trained to school his emotions, he'd have stood there gawking. *Sarge, how do you do it? She must be half your age and a real looker—something you're definitely not.*

"Hi." The velvet-voiced, honey-haired woman crossed the room, her hand extended. "As you probably guessed, Joe stepped out for a moment. He should be back any second." Turquoise eyes welcomed him, and her sincere smile relayed openness. Her fresh looks appealed to him, and when his big hand swallowed her small one, he felt something akin to voltage pass between them. "I'm—"

"Good. You two have met. That'll save me time on introductions." Sergeant Joe Wood stepped through the office door. His large frame dwarfed the petite beauty standing next to Eli. Though a great guy, Sarge had some rough edges. What intrigued the sergeant was obvious—perfect, petite features in a natural presentation and eyes that reminded Eli of the tranquil waters of the Caribbean.

"We haven't actually met," she corrected. "I was just about to introduce myself when you walked in."

As Sarge settled into his squeaky chair, Eli again found himself drinking in all he could of her face. If he ever decided to look for a woman, one like her couldn't be more perfect— small, feminine, and au naturel. But of course he had no plan of ever looking for a woman.

"I'm Delanie Cooper."

He dropped her hand as if it had suddenly transfigured into a poisonous snake. *Delanie? This can't be!* He turned to face Sarge with an accusing stare. "This isn't. . ."

Sarge nodded, confirming Eli's suspicions. "Eli Logan, meet Delanie Cooper, your new partner."

"No way!" Eli moved toward the gray metal desk. He bent over until he and Sarge were eye level. "Absolutely no way!" He glared into Sarge's small, round eyes.

"I told you on the phone you'd been reassigned."

"When you said my new partner was Delanie, I thought you meant like Tony Delaney or Sam Delaney—not Delanie as in a female!" His voice rose, as did his frustration level. "I won't work with another woman." Eli crossed his arms over his chest to underscore the determination of his words.

"You don't have a choice, pal. I call the shots."

"Then I'll go over your head." Eli headed for the door, turning just before his exit. "I'll go all the way to the chief of police if I have to." Reality struck him with a force that stopped him dead in his tracks. "You're Frank Cooper's daughter, aren't you?" He'd heard the chief had one on the force.

Delanie nodded.

So much for plan B. How could he tell his superior he refused to work with his daughter? He glared at Sarge and shook his head. "Why? Why are you doing this? You know how I feel about women cops."

"Delanie is one of the best we have. She's intelligent, quick—"

"She's barely five feet and a hundred pounds. What if I'm wounded and need her to carry me out of the middle of gang crossfire?"

"I know what happened with your last partner." Delanie's velvet voice no longer sounded like a caress; now it just irritated Eli. "But I've never frozen, and I don't think I ever will. I'm strong as an ox and promise I'll work hard not to let you down."

"Have you ever been face-to-face with a forty-five and a guy on the other end who wanted you dead? Let me assure you, talk is cheap." He doubted she'd ever faced more than a routine traffic stop.

"Not only have I looked down a barrel at close range, I took the guy's legs out from under him with a sweep." The two of them stood in a face-off, both refusing to back down. Her eyes lost their serenity and now reminded him of a stormy sea at sunset, but he refused to be impressed by her looks or her claims.

"Eli." Sarge's voice came from right beside Eli, but he didn't break eye contact with Ms. Cooper; she didn't blink an eye either. "Delanie is a black belt in Kajukenbo. She can take care of herself. You, my friend, have a new partner and an assignment that starts tomorrow. You go home now and think long and hard about this decision. Either you show up tomorrow and join Delanie undercover, or you empty your locker, pal." Sarge pushed his way between them and forced their gazes to break.

Anger coursed through Eli like rapids in a river. How could he walk away when this job had been his life for the past ten years? How could he walk away when his sole purpose had become avenging his brother's death by ridding Reno of drug lords?

"I'll be here," he promised, walking to the door. Pausing, he directed his parting words at Delanie. "And you'd better hope you're a good cop, because if you're not, it won't matter whose daughter you are."

His long strides carried him down the narrow hall to the exit. Once outside, he sucked in a huge breath of fresh air. Delanie Cooper had better watch her step, because he'd covered more than one error for Bernadette, and where had that gotten him? He touched his shoulder, remembering.

Slipping on his sunglasses, Eli trekked across the parking lot toward his hog. He'd balked at having a female partner since the day he'd left the academy. He'd watched them, and they weren't as strong or as capable out on the field. Sure, most could shoot well enough; many were better marksmen than he, but they were too emotional for a job that required a cool head and decisive action. Bernadette proved his theory when she forgot her training, gave in to fear, and nearly got him killed.

Eli slipped on his helmet and straddled his bike. Pulling out onto Second, he headed for Virginia Street, making himself a promise: Delanie Cooper wouldn't be the fourth woman on his list to fail him. The next fiasco might cost him his life, and he wasn't willing to pay that high a price. A few mess-ups and he'd be rid of her. Eli Logan never broke promises to anyone, and he wouldn't break this one to himself either.

❧

Delanie glanced from Joe to the door and back again. "Well, your warning that Eli might resent my assignment as his partner now seems a bit understated."

"I told you he had issues." Joe settled back into his chair.

"Issues? The man's a woman-hater." Delanie claimed the green vinyl chair facing Joe.

"He's really a great guy. Has a lot of strength as a cop. Probably one of the best on the force."

"You couldn't prove it by me." Delanie shrugged. "But I don't think I'm the answer to your dilemma. How am I going to help him?" She leaned forward, waiting to hear.

"You're not the answer, Delanie. God is. The police psychologist believes the only way Eli will get past his fear and find true healing is to pair him with a strong, dependable female partner. I chose you because you not only fit the description, but you also have a strong faith in God. You see, I only agree with the psychologist to a point. True healing comes from one source and one source only—God. You can barely get through a sentence without your faith spilling into the conversation. Eli needs a strong dose of what you have to offer."

"That's a big order, Joe. What if I fail him? What if I let him down, too? I'm only human and have lots of room for error."

"I prayed long and hard about finding the right partner for Eli. I'm convinced you're the one for the assignment, so I'll trust that whatever happens is part of God's plan to draw Eli to Himself." Joe tapped his pencil against his desk several times as if to underscore his words.

"I sure hope you're right." Delanie let out a long, slow breath. This assignment looked as if it would be the toughest one she'd had to date. Not the police work, but the friendship evangelism assignment that came with it. How could a woman befriend a woman-hater and lead him to Christ?

God, this one is up to You. I'm willing, but You'll have to handle all the details. And, Lord, I'm sorry I let Eli goad me into a contest of wills. So far on this assignment I've crashed and burned. I failed as a shining light pointing to You.

"I'm going to take off. I'll see you in the morning." Delanie rose and strode to the door. "Do you think he'll be here?"

"Eli—he'll be here, all right. He's a cop through and through. It's all he knows, and frankly, it's his whole life."

The news made Delanie a little sad. Being a police officer was a great job, even a wonderful ministry, but someone's entire life? She needed to know more about Eli. An idea formed.

"Where does he live?"

"Eli?" Joe's wrinkled brow verified his confusion at the abrupt subject change.

"Yeah, Eli." She grinned at Joe's perplexed look.

"What difference does that make?" His brows drew even closer together.

"I want to get a feel for him. Drive through his neighborhood and try to understand this new partner of mine."

"He won't appreciate you snooping around."

"Too bad. He's not willing to sit down with me, get to know me, work out our differences."

"He lives in an apartment—off Ralston just north of I-80."

The news surprised her. "Why? I know the pay's low, but not that low. He could live in a better area than that."

"Two reasons. To keep a pulse on the drug activity in the area and to befriend young boys in his neighborhood, hoping to help keep them off drugs and out of gangs." The admiration in Joe's voice was apparent.

"So Mr. Logan has a caring side." Delanie considered this new information. At least it made him almost human.

"Not for you."

"No, not for me, but at least for someone." She turned to leave; now she had a plan. "See ya," she called over her shoulder on her way out Joe's door.

Delanie took the stairs to the second floor, pondering her new partner. She let out a long breath, feeling overwhelmed by the man. He was so negative, so anti-woman, and yet she couldn't deny the interest she felt, the chemistry when their hands touched. It would take a lot of prayer to maintain a good frame of mind around him.

She popped in to say hi to her dad and obtain more information regarding Mr. Logan. With her other partners, she'd spent time with them over coffee so she could get to know them. That wouldn't be the case here. Whatever she wanted to know, she'd have to ferret out on her own. Her dad said little, except that Eli was a good man and a good cop. He did, however, provide her with Eli's address.

Leaving the precinct, Delanie drove straight to Eli's stomping grounds. After a little searching, she found parking curbside a half block or so from his apartment building—the place Eli called home. It was old and somewhat decrepit, certainly in need of work. Parking down a bit, she smiled as she thought how conspicuous she was in a sports car, even a white one. Hers was not a nondescript surveillance car at all. She watched people come and go. Many were Hispanic and young kids.

Eli exited, wearing sweats and a sleeveless shirt and bouncing a basketball. A group of ten or so boys who looked to be junior high age surrounded him. His hair, almost black and slightly too long, glistened in the sun. Laughter filled the air as he and the boys wrestled over the ball. The scruffy beard that looked like several days' growth still covered his jawline and chin, but somehow it added to his rugged attractiveness. For Delanie, seeing his playful side and watching his interaction with the boys made him all the more appealing.

He glanced in her direction once but apparently didn't see her. Delanie waited until he was a half block away, then followed on foot. At Eleventh Street Eli and his entourage made a left. Delanie jogged to catch up. Unfamiliar with the neighborhood, she had no idea where they were headed.

Just before she rounded the corner where Eli had turned, someone grabbed her from behind. Muscular arms wrapped around her neck and waist, holding her in a choke hold. *Don't panic! Stay calm!* Immediately all of her senses were alert, alive. She sucked hard to take in a breath; the arm across her throat made it difficult. Why hadn't she been paying attention to her surroundings? As a cop, she knew better, especially in this neighborhood. She'd wait. Sooner or later this guy would make a mistake, and she'd make her move. Heart pounding, she prayed for help.

two

"Sarge didn't tell me your nickname was Coop the Snoop."

Eli knew the moment Delanie recognized his voice—some of the tension left her body, and she relaxed a little, but not completely. He loosened his hold the slightest bit, and she inhaled a gulp of air. He didn't want to notice the smell of her—clean with a hint of lavender—or the touch of her—small and soft in his arms—but neither eluded him.

What is it about this woman? He released her, needing to put space between them. She swung around and, using her legs, swept his out from under him. He hit the ground—hard. Dazed, he replayed the last few seconds. One instant he was contemplating her femininity, and the next he was sprawled out on the pavement with a throbbing head and an aching back, listening to a group of boys chuckling somewhere nearby. He'd never hear the end of this from them.

"Man, she's quick," he heard Miguel say.

"Did you see the way she knocked his feet right out from under him?" Oscar asked in a loud whisper.

Delanie reached out her hand to help Eli to his feet. Groaning, he accepted her offer, and she pulled him up. "Don't ever misjudge your opponent." She raised her eyebrow, tilting her chin upward. Turning, she faced the group of boys. "Can anyone play, or is it guys only?"

"Guys only," Eli answered, brushing the dirt off his sweats. He figured he'd cut her off before any of those awestruck teens could invite her into the game.

"But since you're tougher than most of the guys we know"—Miguel shot him a meaningful glance, his brown eyes glowing with mischief—"we can make an exception for you."

"Why, thank you." Delanie dazzled them with a smile that might possibly shame the sun. His little mob of junior high boys surrounded her like bees around a honeycomb, and they walked toward the court while he straggled behind completely forgotten. She joked with them, and they joked back, admiration written across each young face. Great. His little posse abandoned him for the first pretty girl to come along.

"Where do you guys play?" she asked.

"Peavine Elementary," Miguel said, "down on Grandview."

Delanie checked out the yellow school with bright, colorful doors—some blue, green, and red. It looked happy with vines growing up the side of the building, and to her surprise she saw no graffiti. She followed the guys around back to the playground where a full-size basketball court awaited them.

Oscar tossed the basketball to Delanie, and she tossed it to Eli. "Hope you don't mind a girl in the game." Her Caribbean-blue eyes mocked him. She knew he did mind, but she obviously didn't care.

"As long as you're not on my team." He threw the ball back to her—with force. She caught it, and from the slapping sound against her palms, he knew they had to sting, but she didn't even flinch.

Stopping at the edge of the court, Delanie asked, "So whose team am I on?"

"I'll take her," Miguel offered gallantly. She was shorter than most of the boys, so they all knew she was more of a liability than an asset.

"I'll take Eli." Oscar grinned, and Eli knew the chunky boy still pictured him sprawled out on the pavement and could barely contain his laughter. While Miguel and Oscar took turns choosing teams, Eli evaluated his opponent. She'd pulled her hair back into a ponytail, and in her navy tank top, shorts, and tennis shoes, she'd come to play. How did she know he'd be home or even where home was?

Okay, he grudgingly admitted, *she has a cop's nose. And she is spunky—definitely spunky.*

Each team gathered in a circle at opposite ends of the court, discussing strategy, but he only half listened. Delanie Cooper had unquestionably earned an ounce of respect from him today—she was a fast thinker, quick and strong, and he wouldn't underestimate her again, nor would he lose his focus. He'd been thinking of her womanly wiles instead of keeping a clear head. Well, no more. No, sir. He'd pay no more attention to the smell of her, the touch of her, the sound of her, or anything else about her.

Both teams met center court, and Eli flipped a coin. Delanie called heads, and heads it was, so they had the basketball first. His team got into defensive positions while Miguel threw the ball to Delanie. She dribbled down court, weaving through his players. He planted himself between her and the basket. She collided into him, with more force than he expected from someone her size, and lost control of the ball.

Oscar grabbed the loose ball and passed it to Jorge, who dunked it, and they took the lead 2-0. Miguel threw the basketball back in, and Delanie carried it down court again, this time sinking the shot, making the score 2-2. The teams were evenly matched, and the game stayed close. Delanie played tough, and Eli grudgingly noted his admiration had moved up another notch. When they were all drenched with sweat and thoroughly exhausted, they called it quits. His team managed to pull off a three-point victory.

"So now that we've shared a game of hoops, do I get an introduction to your friends?" Delanie asked, walking off the court. She took a gulp of water from the bottle he handed her, and he realized he'd already started taking care of her, watching out for her, even though he'd promised himself not to fall into that role.

"Sure. Guys, this is Delanie Cooper, better known as Coop the Snoop. Coop, the guys."

Delanie rolled her eyes and shook her head, but the smile she shined on him caused his heart to trip over itself. He shifted his gaze away from her. *I won't warm up to her. I will not!*

They all sat in the grass next to the court, chugging water, and each junior higher introduced himself to Delanie. Then they rehashed the best plays of the game. "Did you see the steal Eli made right out of Delanie's hands?"

"Yeah, that was some play, E. A clean lift—all ball." She was actually proud of him, and the thought made him feel warm inside.

He cocked his brow. "E?"

"Hey, if I'm Coop, you're E." She shrugged. "Take it or leave it, dude. It's either Delanie and Eli, Cooper and Logan, or Coop and E."

"Coop and E it is." Eli decided to get her riled. "You know, Coop, for a girl, you don't play half bad." He stretched out on the grass, leaning on his right elbow.

She only laughed. "Thank you. And for a guy, you don't play too bad either—though my brothers would put you to shame."

"Brothers, huh? I knew you had one—Frank Jr."

"Yeah, since Frankie's on the force, I figured you knew him. He's the oldest. Brady is next, then Cody."

"And where do you fall in the lineup?"

She smiled and hung her head. "The baby."

"Three older brothers. Was the word *princess* used in regard to you?"

She blushed and played with a blade of grass. "Occasionally."

"Figures." Eli rose and grabbed his stuff. "Let's head back, guys." He had to keep the distance; they were getting too comfortable, too chummy. His little troop rose, as did Delanie.

"How do you know Eli?" Oscar asked her on the walk back to the apartment building.

"He's my new partner." Delanie glanced at Eli, but he gave no response.

"I figured you for a cop," Miguel said. "How many girls can take guys down unless they're cops?"

The whole herd started laughing. Eli shook his head and rolled his eyes. Nope, he wouldn't live down this humiliation for a long while. Junior high boys had memories a million miles long.

"Have you ever killed anybody?" Oscar wondered.

"Killing people isn't what the job is about. It's about protecting people, and I've protected a lot of people."

Eli thought her answer seemed trite. Of course the *princess* had never killed anybody. He hoped his life never depended on her doing that for him. He'd die for sure. Eli paused at the edge of the road next to his building, his resentment of her returning full force. "You guys head home for lunch and some family time. I want you each to volunteer to do a chore for your moms—an unrequested chore. I'll meet you at three in the clubhouse for a game of pool, but only if your homework and chores are finished."

❧

Eli headed down the driveway toward the back of the complex. She stood on the curb, and he completely ignored her presence. Turning, he took a sidewalk toward the apartments.

"Eli, wait. Can we talk?" Today she'd caught a glimpse of the man he was, but she still hoped to break down some barriers between them.

He paused at his front door. "I have nothing to say." Opening the door, he faced her with one foot inside the apartment and the other on the outside mat. "Look, Delanie. Get this straight—I don't want to be your friend, your buddy, or even your partner. And I certainly don't ever want you showing up here again." His tone was even and matter-of-fact. "You got it?"

Delanie's spirits sank, but she wouldn't let him see the discouragement. Raising her chin a fraction, she said with determination, "With all my other partners—"

"I'm not all your other partners." He'd raised his volume a tad. "We're not having coffee. We're not having lunch. We're not having a conversation—not now, not ever!" He paused and shook his head. "What about this don't you get? I've been completely clear, haven't I?"

Delanie nodded. "Will you be at work tomorrow?" His words made her doubt he'd keep the job if it meant an assignment with her.

"I guess you'll have to wait and see." Eli slammed the door behind him.

Shoulders drooping, Delanie ambled to her car, kicking a pebble along the way. Climbing in, she buckled her seat belt and leaned her head against the bucket seat. "Lord, I feel so hurt. I've never had anyone so blatantly dislike me." The worst part was, she really wanted to be his friend. Closing her eyes, she sighed. No, the worst part was, she found him so attractive, so appealing—so manly.

"And he hates me." She'd hoped that someday he'd see God could rescue him from his lonely life, teach him about joy, lead him to peace. Not just because Joe wanted her to impact him for Christ, but also because he mattered to her.

She started her car and shifted into first. "Wonder what he'd do if I showed up for pool?" She laughed at the thought. He'd probably have her arrested for stalking him. "I'm going to make this guy like me if it's the last thing I do. People always like me." She let out the clutch, and the car rolled forward. He wouldn't be the first person to reject her friendship. Her pride wouldn't stand for that.

&

The next morning Eli headed out the door early for his meeting with Sarge, where he'd get his next assignment. Hopping on his hog, he caught Virginia Street to downtown and took a left on Second. Parking his bike in the police lot, he caught sight of Delanie walking toward the two-story building. He didn't call out to her but avoided her presence as long as possible. She'd been on his mind all night—her smile, her warmth, her openness, even when he bordered on rude. Letting out a long, slow breath, he reminded himself that he didn't need her complicating his life. Besides, eventually every relationship ended in pain—they always did. He was living proof.

Eli took the narrow hall to Sarge's office. At least he'd be back on the streets, making a difference. He may be stuck with Delanie Cooper, but even having her as an albatross couldn't stop him from making arrests, busting dealers, and getting illegal substances off the street.

He rapped on the open door once. Delanie and Sarge looked up. "Eli, come in." Sarge rose and motioned him forward. Eli took the vinyl chair next to Delanie but never glanced in her direction. The scent of lavender, however, teased his nose with an awareness of her presence.

Sarge walked over and shut the door, handing them both a copy of the case file. Eli flipped it open. The words *Baby-Selling Ring* jumped off the page. He glanced at Sarge, who was studying him. Eli shut the folder, stood, and dropped it on the desk. "There must be some mistake. I'm assigned to the drug detail. You've got the wrong guy." Eli experienced a mixture of fear and anger—fear that they'd taken him off his regular unit and anger at their nerve.

"Delanie's the perfect cop for this assignment—"

"And she can have this assignment. I want to go back to the drug detail."

"Eli, sit down." Sarge used his no-nonsense tone. "Your old unit is full right now, and Delanie needs a partner. You, pal, need an assignment. It all works."

Eli dropped into the chair. "Not for me, it doesn't."

"I'm not fighting you on this one." Sarge leaned forward. "Are you in or out?"

"From what you said yesterday. . ." Eli stared at his fist in his lap. "I either accept this position and this partner, or I'm out of a job." He felt the urge to punch something. "I have a dad to support. I don't have a choice."

"Then will you try to remember that and stop butting heads with me at every turn?" Sarge handed the file back to Eli and cleared his throat. Then he put on his reading glasses and opened his copy of the case. "Delanie will pose as a pregnant teen, and you're the father of her child. She wants to keep the baby, but you're pressuring her into selling the child for money because you're out of work. Delanie's appearance makes her ideal. Not only do they have hope for a beautiful baby, but she can easily pass for a teen."

"Thanks a lot." Delanie spoke for the first time that morning.

"Someday you'll be happy—" Sarge began.

"You sound like my mother. Someday I'll be happy I look twelve when I'm actually twenty-eight."

Eli hadn't guessed she was that old. He'd have said twenty-four at the max, but Sarge hit the looks part dead-on. Delanie Cooper was one pretty lady. This morning she wore jeans that accentuated her small frame and a pink T-shirt that emphasized her slender waist. *Stop! You're thinking about her again.* Eli reopened the folder and focused on the task before him.

"Not twelve, but sixteen," Sarge assured her. "We'll set you up with a fake belly, maternity clothes, IDs. Both of your histories are in the folder." He held his up. "One thing." He looked at Eli. "You're a young couple who's in love, so you'll have to play the part. The animosity between you two must be gone. Just like in the drug world, Eli, you've got to be one hundred percent believable."

Great. Now we have to be lovey-dovey. The assignment got worse with every tick of the clock. If he didn't have this wall of hostility raised between them, how could he keep his distance? She'd already been popping up in his head; all he needed was her taking root in his heart. No, this news was not good at all.

"We've been working on this case for a while, to no avail. As you know, baby selling is still a misdemeanor in most states—fortunately no longer here. We've finally figured out we'll have to infiltrate the ring from the inside since we haven't been able to penetrate from the outside. Thus the need for you two. We believe a doctor and lawyer have teamed up on this venture and are making a fortune. We have several possible suspects, but nothing concrete. You two have a lot of work cut out for you."

"How do you even know the ring exists if you have so little evidence, and why are you suddenly willing to put two full-time cops on the job?" Eli asked.

"Murder. A young teen disappeared, and we treated it as a runaway. She was only thirteen years old. The information is in your packet." Sarge waved the folder in the air. "About four months later she placed a call to her mother saying she was pregnant and some people were giving her a lot of money for her baby. Problem was, she no longer wanted the money; she wanted to keep her baby. Before her mother could get any substantial information, she heard a ruckus, and the line went dead. The girl's body was discovered last week. From the autopsy we know she'd given birth just hours before her death."

Eli felt sick. A thirteen-year-old kid—not old enough to be a mom—certainly not old enough to die. He shook his head, and some of the pain from his brother's death punched him in the gut. Teen deaths because of crime—any crime—had to be stopped. He flipped through the file until he found her picture. Julie Johnson stared back at him with blue eyes and curly blond hair. He'd never forget her face.

Sarge and Delanie were talking, but he'd missed the gist of the conversation. "Sound okay to you, Eli?" Sarge asked.

Eli must have looked lost. Delanie said to him, "We'll go look over the file and come back this afternoon for the final briefing."

Eli nodded.

"How about if we head for Dreamer's? I haven't had my morning caffeine yet," she said.

Not into the popular coffeehouses, he was a simple guy who liked simple things like good old Folger's. "Whatever."

"Do you want to walk? It's easier than searching for parking."

He shrugged. They bid Sarge farewell and agreed to meet back in his office at three. In the meantime he and Delanie had a lot of work ahead of them.

She led the way down the drab hall and out into the morning sunshine. They walked in silence along the Raymond I. Smith Truckee River Walk. Following the waterway, they trekked the few blocks to the old red brick building housing Dreamer's Coffeehouse and Deli on the corner of Virginia and the river walk.

"I love the river—something about the sound of the water. . ." Stopping, she inhaled the fragrance of the flowers planted along the way. "The pastoral setting never fails to lift my mood."

Delanie ordered a hot latte, and he ordered plain coffee—black.

They found a corner table and spread out their files, what they could. The little round table didn't allow much room for spreading. He watched her thumb through the paperwork until she came to the girl's picture. She pulled it out and just stared for the longest time. He watched the emotions on her face; this case had become personal to her, too. Something about that young face in the photograph—the face that would never go to a prom, never get a driver's license, never grow old. . .

Delanie let out a long, slow breath and laid the picture on top of her paperwork. "Sometimes life isn't fair."

At least they agreed on something. "Seldom, if ever, is life fair."

Delanie studied him for a moment. He refocused on the case notes, not wishing to continue the conversation or the scrutiny.

Clearing her throat, Delaine said, "Joe thought the first thing we should do is choose names we'll both remember and respond to easily. I was thinking maybe Ethan for you, and I can still call you E, but it's your call."

"Ethan's fine."

"What about me?"

Eli shook his head, still not wanting to think about her.

"How about Coopet?" she asked with a grin. She must be trying to be silly to pull him out of his funk. "Or Coopetta?"

In spite of himself, he smiled. "You could be D, and I'll be E."

"Sure, and how about F for our last name?" She rolled her eyes, and they both chuckled. Laughter kept all cops sane, making the job bearable and releasing tension. Man, did she look beautiful when she laughed. He thought about what name might fit her, something fairly close to her own, something soft and feminine.

"How about Lanie?"

Her expression changed at his suggestion, but he couldn't quite read her. "Lanie?" she asked quietly.

"Lanie." This time he said it with absolute certainty.

three

Lanie. Pain squeezed Delanie's heart. At her insistence, everyone had stopped calling her Lanie when she was ten— right after Grandpa died. Hearing it now—after all those years—still brought a reaction. She'd been Grandpa's special girl, and Lanie was his special name for her. He'd started the trend, and soon the whole family followed his lead.

"Coop?" Eli's tone reflected his uncertainty. "If you don't like Lanie..." His brow creased.

She shook her head. He seemed so pleased with the idea; she didn't want to spoil what little progress they'd made. "Lanie's fine." Inhaling a deep breath, she pulled a highlighter from her purse and began to read the case file, avoiding his probing eyes, not wishing him to see the emotion the name evoked. They sat in silence, sipping their hot beverages, studying the notes, and occasionally commenting on something from the file.

A couple of hours later, Delanie stood, stretched, and turned her head to loosen the kinks in her neck. "I'm getting hungry. I don't eat breakfast, so by midmorning I'm always famished. Do you like Mexican food?"

Eli glanced from his paperwork to his watch, then up at her. "Sure, but at 10:00 a.m.?" His expression seemed to question her sanity.

"By the time we walk over there and order, and they cook everything, it'll be almost eleven." She tried to convince him of the common sense of her plan. "Eleven is lunchtime, right?"

"I suppose." He rose from his chair.

"Do you mind?" At his shrug Delanie scooped up her case notes and filed them back in the folder. He followed her lead. She grabbed her purse off the back of the chair and headed for the door, depositing her empty cup in the trash on the way out. Eli held the door for her.

"Ever been to Bertha Miranda's?" she asked.

"Down Mill?" Eli asked as he shot a basket with his cup, hitting the outdoor container dead center.

"Yep." Delanie raised her face to the warm Nevada sun, and they started their little jaunt toward one of Reno's older eating establishments.

"Never been there. I've heard the food's great, but the wait is always so long that I never bothered."

"Don't you know the best things in life are worth the wait?" She studied his profile—the strong jawline and chiseled cheekbone. He made no response to her comment, verbal or otherwise, so she continued, "Anyway, all your info is correct, which is why now is the perfect time to go. My family comes here often after church on Sundays. We make it a point to arrive early and then dash to a table when the doors open. So your job is to mow down anyone who gets in our way. My brothers have it down to a science."

"If I'm the mower, what's your job?"

"To apologize for your rude behavior."

Eli chuckled. Not quite a laugh, but a chuckle nonetheless. The sound quickened her heart. Maybe she was winning him over. They veered left at Mill.

"Now that you're Ethan and I'm Lanie, where do you think we should start? Obviously not with a doctor since I'm not actually pregnant. He might catch on rather quickly that we're phonies." Delanie laid her hand against her flat stomach, wondering what she'd look like with a protruding belly.

"I've been weighing our possibilities all morning, and I think we should start with a stakeout of the list of suspected lawyers' offices, figure out who's getting a lot of visits from pregnant teens. We'll pinpoint any expecting couples, follow them, and start up a conversation. You work on the women—I'll take the men."

Delanie nodded. "Ask pointed questions and share our story."

"Exactly."

They joined about fifteen or twenty other soon-to-be diners waiting out front for the restaurant to open. Both grew quiet, knowing it was inappropriate to discuss a case within earshot of others. Delanie had an idea and decided to proceed with their role-playing. They'd have to practice to be believable as a young couple expecting a child. She crossed her arms over her midsection. "How can you even consider giving up your own flesh and blood?"

A stunned expression crossed Eli's face before understanding settled in. "I don't have a job; we'll soon be homeless. How can you consider bringing a baby into this rotten situation?"

She thought about Julie Johnson losing not only her baby, but her life. Tears sprang to her eyes, which was exactly what she'd hoped for. Patting her stomach in a maternal way, she said, "Love is all a baby really needs."

"Lanie, what planet are you from? Babies also need diapers, formula, and a dry place to live." Eli's voice rose with each declaration.

By now the crowd had grown silent. Most eyes were on them. Tears rolled down Delanie's cheeks. She turned her back on Eli and crossed her arms again.

Unexpectedly Eli slipped his arms around her from behind and nuzzled the side of her neck with his scruffy chin. Thrill-chills shot through her all the way to her toes. "Don't cry, baby. It'll be okay." He spoke softly, tenderly. "We'll figure something out. Please don't cry." Her knees felt like noodles, and she leaned against him for support.

He turned her in his arms and planted a kiss on her lips. Her heart beat as if she'd jogged five miles at a quick pace. Dazed, Delanie couldn't believe this was happening or how much she enjoyed his arms and his kiss. She stood staring into his face, trying to discern the emotions she saw there, trying to discern her own emotions.

As quickly as he'd swept her into his arms, she backed away from him. "Our audience is gone." Delanie glanced around; she and Eli were the only two left waiting next to the rock wall. Everyone else had entered the restaurant through the double wooden doors. Her face grew warm.

She lowered her head and led the way into the restaurant, keeping her eyes on the floor tile. Luckily a table in the back remained open. Instead of taking her seat, she said, "Excuse me a moment." Not even glancing in Eli's direction, she quickly made her way to the restroom, hoping to compose herself. Once inside, Delanie leaned against the wall and covered her hot cheeks with her palms. *What's wrong with me? I cannot be attracted to him. I can't! But I am.* Staring in the mirror, she wished she could erase the "wide-eyed girl with stardust in her eyes" look.

❧

Eli sucked in a deep breath. When he'd decided to toy with Delanie, he hadn't realized the way it would affect him. Her innocence was obvious, and he knew she hailed from a staunch Christian family; so when he assumed her naive in the ways of a man and a woman, he'd been right. Her kiss was shy and uncertain. This girl wasn't worldly wise. The stunned expression etched on her face at the end of the kiss spoke volumes, and she couldn't get out of his arms fast enough.

What shocked him was his own response. He'd enjoyed holding her, but even more startling, he had the urge to hold her forever—and he wasn't a forever kind of guy. He shook his head to rid himself of the thought. *Delanie Cooper, I won't let you get to me.*

When she returned, he stood and pulled out the wooden chair with the padded seat. "You okay?"

"Fine." Her answer was short and clipped—her cheeks still flushed.

He took the chair to Delanie's right. Fairly certain their kiss had affected her even more than it had him, he decided he'd play it up and kiss her at every opportunity. Maybe then she'd ditch him and this job, and he could go back to his old unit, far away from her and those wide aquamarine eyes.

Taking her hand in his, he leaned over, kissed her cheek, and whispered in her ear, "Remember what Sarge said about being 100 percent believable as a young couple in love?"

Delanie nodded but remained tense. He smiled. His plan was working already.

"You're not playing your part very well," he mocked, placing a light kiss on her very kissable mouth.

She gave him a dirty look and picked up her menu. "I'm still mad at you for even suggesting we sell the baby." She pushed him away. "Don't act all ooey-gooey like that never happened."

The waitress arrived, and Delanie ordered the ground beef tacos. Eli followed her lead.

"Good job on the mad girlfriend role," Eli said softly.

"Let's talk about something else besides selling our baby, something more pleasant, or how about nothing at all?" Sarcasm laced her tone.

"Fine," Eli ground out. He needed to think anyway. Could he overdose Delanie on affection without risking himself? Every touch filled him with a longing for more. A longing for things he'd ages ago accepted he'd never have, never even wanted until now. Delanie Cooper made him wonder if his decision had been so easy because no woman had ever brought his senses to life the way she did.

The waitress set two plates in front of them, and they ate their lunch in silence. Delanie seemed to have as many uncertainties as he faced, though he was sure his touch had repulsed her—a much different response from his own.

After lunch they walked back to the police station not too far north of the restaurant. They found an empty interrogation room and spread out their files on a long table. Delanie settled in on one side, so Eli took the chair across from her.

"You think we should start with a stakeout?" She still hadn't made eye contact since the kiss.

Eli nodded, forcing her to look up.

"Tomorrow at nine?" She bit her bottom lip.

He nodded again, noting the vulnerability in her eyes.

Delanie flipped through the paperwork. "One of the suspects is in a downtown lawyers' office. Do you want to meet here or there?"

"Whatever," he said with a shrug.

Sarge rapped on the door once and joined them.

"How's the strategy coming?" He took the seat next to Delanie.

Eli filled him in on their plan of action.

"Sounds great. I knew the two of you would figure out something." Sarge pulled his cell phone out of his shirt pocket, hit a number on the face of the phone, and put the tiny thing to his ear. He made arrangements for a car to be delivered the next morning for Eli and Delanie to use during the case. Standing, he said, "At 0800. I'll see you then." He exited, leaving them alone.

Eli stared at Delanie. The reality of their situation hit him dead-on. Could she protect him if the need arose?

"What?" she asked. "Are you hoping if you stare long enough, I'll vanish?"

He ignored her remark. "Someone in this ring owns a gun and isn't afraid to use it."

"I know." Her expression grew solemn.

He rose and leaned over the table, taking an in-your-face stance. "Do you? Do you know? Can I count on you, Coop? This is a lot more than proving you can do whatever a guy can. Our lives are at stake. They killed at least one girl, and if we get too close, we might be their next target. Can you kill someone if you have to?"

Her face turned white. She closed her eyes and drew in a deep breath. Panic rose inside Eli until he thought it might choke the breath out of him.

"I can't be out there tomorrow with someone who's afraid. You need to get off this case right now!" Eli laid his right hand across his left shoulder. "I won't go out there with another coward."

Delanie rose and glared at him. "Your opinion of women is awfully low. Not all of us are cowards."

"I saw the fear, Delanie, written all over your face!" Eli was now yelling.

"I'm not afraid of my gun, nor am I afraid to use it," she assured him in a hushed tone.

"You can't deny the terror I saw with my own eyes."

"Yeah, I'm afraid, Eli." She hung her head for a quiet moment. When she raised it, he saw fire in her eyes. "Afraid I'll have to kill another person. Afraid someone else will die because I'm doing my job." Her voice cracked with emotion, and she turned away from him.

Is she saying she's already killed someone?

Before the words came out of his mouth, she was speaking again. This time there was no denying the pain woven through each word. "I've already killed someone, Eli—a nineteen-year-old kid in a convenience store robbery. He pointed a gun at the clerk, and I shot him." She sucked in a ragged breath and faced him. "Are you happy? Does that knowledge make you feel safer with me? Is that what you want—to know your partner has already shot and killed another human being?"

Sparks shot from her eyes. "I am not some women's libber trying to prove I can do anything a man can do. I feel lucky to have been born in America—land of the free. I love this country. I love this city. What I do has nothing to do with proving anything. I just want to keep people safe. I want to keep another thirteen-year-old kid from living Julie Johnson's nightmare."

Delanie stuffed her paperwork into the folder. Her hand shook slightly. She looked him square in the eyes. "So don't you worry, Eli Logan. If I have to kill someone to keep you alive, I will. And I'll hate the fact every day for the rest of my life."

She grabbed her purse and threw it over her shoulder. At the door she turned to face him. "I think you're the one with the problem. You have some vendetta to prove that every female cop is incompetent. If I were a man, would you be having all these doubts? I think not! I'm sick of getting no respect because I'm a woman, because I'm small, because I'm the chief's daughter, or because I'm not ugly. I'm a good cop, Detective Logan, and if you don't believe it now, you will when we're finished with this case." She jerked the door open, then slammed it behind her.

For several seconds Eli could only stare at the door, trying to process everything she'd said. He shook his head, gathered his things, and headed down the hall to Sarge's office. The door stood ajar. Eli knocked once. Sarge glanced up from his paperwork.

"Why didn't you tell me?" Eli moved toward the green vinyl chair.

"Tell you what?" Sarge shuffled through the pile of papers.

"Why didn't you tell me Delanie had shot someone? Do you know what a fool I made of myself?"

Sarge shrugged. "I figured she'd tell you, if and when she wanted you to know." He pulled a manila envelope from one of his desk drawers. "Take these home and read them. I want them back in the morning."

Eli reached for the envelope.

"See you at eight—and close my door, will you?" Sarge dismissed him.

Eli did as he was told, heading back to the interrogation room he'd recently vacated. He dumped the contents of the envelope onto the folding table. Several newspaper articles spilled out—every one about Delanie Cooper and her heroic actions in the robbery. She'd received a citation from the department and was labeled a hero.

Great. Not only was she beautiful, appealing, and intelligent; now he also had to recognize her abilities as a cop. He didn't want to like her or respect her or admire her, but in two days she'd managed to make him guilty of all three.

And tomorrow her presence would wreak havoc on his already confused emotions.

four

Shaking with anger, Delanie left Eli to draw his own conclusions. She practically ran to her car—escaping the man who caused her emotions to soar to heights and then drop to valleys she'd never known before. And all in the span of a few short hours.

She hopped into her little car, opened the sunroof, and hoped the wind would carry her woes away. Gulping deep breaths, she wanted to exhale the anger she'd allowed to overcome her. Taking the on-ramp, she shifted into fifth and merged onto I-80.

"I'm sorry, God." She blew out a noisy breath. "I can't remember the last time I've been that mad." But somehow she knew that the handful of times she'd been truly livid, work was always at the center. More precisely, someone questioning her ability as a cop. "How long will it take? I've been doing the job well for six years, yet no one believes I can."

Exiting at McCarran Boulevard, she followed a pickup until she hung a left at Mayberry Drive. A couple of blocks later she pulled into Mayberry Townhomes. She'd grown to love living alone. Well—almost alone. Hank, a retired police dog, and Junie B. Jones, a miniature beagle, resided with her. Or perhaps they allowed her to reside with them.

Thinking of her two buddies made her smile, and some of the anger dissipated. Delanie turned into her garage under the two-story town house and heard Junie's welcoming yelp.

Junie and Hank would be waiting impatiently to greet her. She climbed the stairs inside her garage that led to her utility room. True to form, her dogs greeted her with wagging tails and leashes in their mouths as she entered the house. Dropping her purse on the washing machine, she knelt and scratched both dogs behind their ears. Hank rolled over on his back for a belly rub. Delanie grabbed both leashes and flung them over one shoulder.

"How did you two know it's time for our jog?" Delanie asked, starting toward the bedroom. Both of her furry roommates followed. She quickly changed her clothes, tied the laces of her running shoes, and snapped the two leashes onto the dog collars. Junie always made a game of the task, dancing and dodging her master as if she dreaded the daily jog. Once outside, Delanie did a few stretches, loosening her tight muscles. Today she needed the run more than most days and started at a quick pace, hoping to de-stress and decompress.

She always ran down South McCarran to Coughlin Ranch. The upscale housing community featured several jogging trails and nature walks, giving the impression of leaving "the biggest little city in the world" a million miles behind. While out there with her dogs and God, she could forget the casinos, the crime, and maybe even Eli. This was her time alone to focus on her Lord and the wonderful world He'd created.

At the end of her jog, Delanie followed her daily ritual of dropping by her parents' house. Her mom always gave her "granddogs" a biscuit and Delanie a glass of water. They'd visit for fifteen or twenty minutes while Marilyn Cooper started dinner. Some nights Delanie would stay and join them; but Tuesday nights she always ate with a group of her friends, and then they'd all go to the singles' Bible study together.

Delanie sat at the bar on the edge of her mother's kitchen, watching her peel carrots. "Mom, what makes one man's kiss so different from another's?"

"The shape and skill of his lips." Her brow was raised, and she wore a deadpan expression.

Delanie rolled her eyes at her mom's quick wit. "No, I mean the reaction we as women have inside."

Her mom laid down her peeler. "I'm no expert, but I think it's that old mystery called chemistry." She drew her brows together in an attempted stern look. "And whom have you been kissing?"

"Believe me, no one I want to be kissing, at least not the sane, down-to-earth side of me." Delanie took a sip of water before expounding. She filled her mom in on the events of the past two days. "But when he took me in his arms and his lips met mine, there was no place on earth I'd rather have been."

"Honey." Her mom's tone rang with parental concern. "Be careful. You're skating on thin ice."

Delanie nodded—that much she'd already figured out.

Her mother continued. "I don't believe in "missionary dating," going out with a guy to 'save his soul.' Only once in my life have I ever seen it work out. Most of the time it ends in heartache and sometimes disaster."

"I know." Delanie glanced at her watch. "I've got to run, Mom. I'm supposed to meet the girls in barely an hour." She jumped up, opened the sliding glass door, and whistled for her dogs. They'd been out back, playing with her parents' black lab, Rambo.

She kissed her mom's cheek and headed for the entry hall. "I'll be praying, honey!" her mom hollered as Delanie shut the front door.

An hour later, after taking a quick shower and feeding her dogs, Delanie pulled into Mayberry Landing—a casual galleria filled with boutiques. Because of its name, the place always reminded her of the Andy Griffith reruns she'd watched with her grandparents as a child, though much more upscale than his town had been. She parked in front of Walden's Coffeehouse. The quaint mini-mall also carried her far away from her job and downtown Reno.

Entering the wood-planked coffeehouse, she saw Jodi, Kristen, and Courtney already seated at their usual corner spot with their dinners in front of them. On her way to the table, she stopped at the counter and ordered a hot veggie wrap and a mocha ole to drink.

As she approached the table, she heard Courtney say, "He kissed me."

"Not you, too." Delanie sat in the last remaining chair. "Who kissed you?"

"Dr. Gorgeous," Kristen interjected. She shoved a long strand of chestnut hair behind her ear.

"Wait." Jodi pointed at Delanie. "You said, 'Not you, too.' Does that mean you were kissed today, as well?" She scrunched her forehead, her dark brows pulling together. "Spill."

Delanie decided to dodge the moment as long as possible, not even sure why she'd said anything. "Sounds like I arrived right in the middle of a kiss between Courtney and Dr. Gorgeous. Let her finish, and then I'll tell you my saga about me and Detective Dangerous."

"Detective Dangerous sounds simply dreamy, dahling." Courtney winked at Delanie. "But I'm certain he can't compete with my gorgeous doctor whose kiss sends me into orbit." Courtney used a corny accent, and they all laughed at her antics.

"Do tell us the tale of the gorgeous doctor and the nurse who's been swept off her feet by a single heart-stopping kiss." Kristen was always the romantic.

Courtney blushed. "Who said anything about a single kiss?"

"You kissed him more than once?" Amazement tinged Jodi's question. "How well do you know this guy?"

Kristen cocked her head. "Better than she did yesterday."

"Let's rewind," Delanie said. "I missed the beginning of this story, and I'm going to need a recap. So please, nobody say a word until I get back with my dinner." The guy who took her order had just called her name, and her food waited on the edge of the counter.

Delanie returned to the table and took a sip of her hot mocha, loving the soothing feel of the liquid sliding down her throat. Between her fast but hot shower and the warmth of her beverage, she'd finally relaxed some after her exchange with Eli a few hours prior.

"Do tell, Courtney, and start at the beginning." Courtney reminded Delanie of a model—tall, long, and lean. Her blond hair was always perfect, never a strand out of place, and her blue eyes resembled the sky on a clear day. Courtney never lacked for male attention.

"We have a new doc who just transferred into intensive care. He is such a hunk, and he's into me!" She made the statement as if it were a big surprise.

"Duh! They're always into you, Courtney," Jodi reminded her, shaking her shoulder-length brunette hair in exasperation.

Courtney daintily ran her hand over her sunshine-hued locks, and her beguiling smile showcased perfect teeth. "That is *so* not true. I've been trying for months to get Pastor Paul's attention. He never even notices me, so I'm moving on." It was an honest assessment. He seemed to be the one man on earth who was unaware of her, and his indifference made Courtney want him all the more.

Delanie asked, "How long has Dr. Gorgeous been on staff at St. Mary's?"

"He started yesterday." Courtney studied her napkin as she rolled it up into a tiny wad and avoided eye contact with any of her friends. She surely knew they'd disapprove. They'd been down this road with her before—numerous times. Men were Courtney's weakness, and no matter how many times she tried, she couldn't seem to remain objective or Christ-centered when a new guy strolled into her life.

Delanie held her tongue. How could she say a word about kissing a man she barely knew when she'd done that very thing earlier today? But honestly, she would have loved to give Courtney a good shake.

Jodi, however, had no qualms. "You made out with a man you've only known two days! What happened to the commitment we each made at the singles' conference last month? We all agreed to get to know men as friends *before* we let the physical aspect get in the way and confuse the issue." Jodi's brown eyes held a challenge as she glanced from Courtney to Delanie.

Delanie knew Jodi's message was directed at both her and Courtney. Guilt stabbed at Delanie's heart. She released a long, slow, audible breath. Eyeing each of her friends around the table, she knew they'd be disappointed in her, as well.

"And who kissed you?" Jodi's expression was confused. "I didn't even know you were dating."

"I'm not," Delanie mumbled, mentally preparing for her turn at the stake.

Kristen chimed in, "I just saw you at church on Sunday. You also met someone in two days?" She played with her large hoop earring.

"It was work—part of an undercover assignment." Delanie knew her justification sounded weak and pathetic.

Courtney said nothing. She'd spent an inordinate amount of time stirring her soup, not even glancing up. Her feelings were probably hurt; but truth be told, if this wasn't a repeated pattern, they'd all have been more supportive and less judgmental.

Two curious friends tossing out questions a mile a minute brought Delanie back to the present. She briefly gave them an overview of the past two days.

"So the kiss meant nothing to you—just an unpleasant job assignment?" Kristen raised her brows.

Delanie felt her face grow warm. "Therein lies the problem—it wasn't as unpleasant as I wish it had been."

Courtney made eye contact and smiled. "Boy, girlfriend, do I know what you mean. Heart-stopping, orbit-sending, incredible. I couldn't stop at just one—didn't even want to." Her face flushed with her excitement, and her gaze rested on Jodi, daring her to say another word.

Delanie shrugged. "Eli's kiss was amazing, but I don't want to kiss him, not ever again. He's not a Christian, and I can't risk falling for him. The attraction is already there, but I know I've got to be firm in my resolve. The pleasure of his kiss isn't worth risking my future. I want a husband like my dad—a guy sold out to the Lord—and I want a father like that for my kids."

Both Jodi and Kristen nodded in agreement.

Courtney spoke up. "But if he has feelings for you, maybe he'll start going to church, hear about God, and give his life to Jesus."

Delanie wondered at that moment if Dr. Gorgeous didn't follow Christ and Courtney was only justifying her relationship.

"That never works." Jodi's statement was filled with certainty. "Look at all the kids from our days in the college group who made that decision. Many of them ended up compromising their beliefs and their convictions."

Courtney glared at Jodi. "You're always so sure of your walk, but maybe this time you're wrong." She raised her chin, daring any of them to question her wisdom. "He told me if I'd go out with him tonight, he'd come to church with me on Sunday."

Delanie's heart sank, and she had to speak up. "You know it's a risk at best. Don't you think Dr. Gorgeous is used to sleeping with his dates?"

"No. And you should know I won't do that!" Courtney's glare shifted to Delanie.

"Courtney," Kristen said, "he's a thirty-something-year-old man who lives in our modern world. In today's society it's more accepted and even expected by many. You know that—we all know that."

"Court." Jodi's sad eyes pleaded with Courtney to listen. "You've already come close a few times with Christian guys. If you're attracted to this doctor fellow, and he has the experience we suspect, how will you resist? He'll probably know just what he's doing and how to make a girl putty in his hands. I know you get mad at me for always telling it like it is, but I don't want you to fall. I don't want you to settle. I care about you."

Courtney rose. "I'm not arguing with you guys about this. I've made up my mind. I'm dating Tad, and I will not compromise my moral standards—not one bit!" She picked up her tea glass and soup bowl. "Now if you'll excuse me,

I have a date with a gorgeous man, so I won't be at Bible study tonight."

As Delanie watched Courtney leave the coffee shop, she fought a huge urge to run after her, tackle her, and beg her not to go.

"No, he isn't affecting her decisions, not one bit. She hasn't missed Bible study in over a year, until tonight. . ." Kristen voiced what they were all thinking.

Delanie shook her head. "I need you guys to pray for me. I'm in the same predicament. Only it's my job assignment, so I have no option. Eli and I will be spending eight or more hours a day together, and I realize how vulnerable that makes me."

"So his kiss was pretty amazing, huh?"

Delanie smiled at Kristen. "You have no idea. When he slipped his arms around me, I felt like a bowl of jelly. At that moment every rational thought fled, and all I wanted was to kiss him. The only good thing is that I don't affect him at all— except maybe he feels disgust."

"So he won't be trying to date you?" Jodi asked.

Delanie chuckled. "When pigs fly—and believe me, I do see the blessing in that."

"That may be God's protection," Kristen agreed.

"I've decided to ask him to refrain from kissing me because of my religious convictions. We can play the loving couple without quite so much intimacy." Delanie raised her chin in determination. "There will be no more lip-locking with Detective Dangerous—absolutely none! I promise you guys that."

❧

Eli strapped on his helmet, sat astride his bike, and cranked the engine to life. Riding home, he couldn't get his mind off Delanie, her heroics, or the mayhem she inflicted on his emotions. Tuesday and Thursday nights he tutored his junior high posse, and he was running late. He attempted to focus on them and their educational needs, but Delanie kept sneaking into his thoughts. When he rode up to his apartment, the whole gang—all eight of them—were waiting for him in the parking lot. Removing his helmet, they loaded into his old, dingy-white, fifteen-passenger van—the one he'd bought just for toting them—and they headed for the nearby Burger House.

Oscar grabbed the other bucket seat in the front, and Miguel sat in the center of the seat right behind them. "So, Eli, how's that fine partner of yours?" Miguel asked in a teasing tone, and all of the boys chuckled.

Eli gave him "the look" through the rearview mirror, but he'd obviously lost his power of persuasion.

"She swept you off your feet again?" one of the boys from the very back hollered. The chuckles increased to loud laughter.

"Glad you boys can have fun with that whole incident." Eli knew their banter would be ongoing for the next few months, and he took no offense. He'd have done the same at their age.

"She's sure pretty," Oscar said in low tones for Eli's hearing only.

He smiled at the boy and nodded. "Too pretty. Girls like her get us boys into trouble."

"Whatcha mean?" Oscar asked.

Eli thought carefully about his answer. He didn't want his negative opinion to taint their young minds.

"She's the kind of girl to make a man think about marriage, and because of my job, I decided long ago that I'd never marry."

"But lots of cops are married." Oscar shot a hole in Eli's excuse.

"I know, but since I do undercover work, it's more dangerous. And I have my dad and you guys. My life doesn't have room for a wife." Only the empty ache in his heart belied his words.

When they arrived at the restaurant, Eli stepped to the end of the line, surrounded by his noisy band of boys. An obviously pregnant teen and a man in a suit were in another line, a couple of people ahead of where Eli stood, but they caught his eye. The hair on his neck stood on end. He studied them, straining to pick up bits of conversation. *If only these boys would be quiet.*

"How about if you guys go grab a couple of tables? I pretty much know what you want anyhow since your orders never change."

The rowdy group boisterously made their way to a spot in the corner. Eli focused on the odd couple in line, trying to figure out if the young woman was with her father or perhaps someone connected to the baby-selling ring. Tilting his head, he tried to catch their words, but the fast-food establishment was too loud, even with his boys across the restaurant.

After receiving their order, the man grabbed the bag in one hand and the girl's elbow with his other. As they passed Eli, he heard her say, "That's a lot of money." She wore a surprised but pleased expression. Eli resisted the urge to grab her from him then and there. For all he knew, they could be discussing her allowance, though he doubted it.

They exited out the side door. Eli darted to the back of the restaurant. "You guys stay put for two minutes." Eight pairs of startled eyes fixed on him, but he had no time to explain. He rushed for the door but caught no sign of the pair. He ran around the building to the other side. Still nothing. *How could they vanish into thin air?*

five

Eli entered Sarge's office at seven forty-five the next morning, and there stood a very pregnant-appearing Delanie. He stopped short—the scene before him felt intimate, something he wanted no part of. She had her hands under the false belly, which only highlighted her "condition," but it was the yearning he felt that nearly sent him running. He thought he'd settled the issue of family long ago.

"Eli," Sarge said, "you're early."

He nodded, but his eyes hadn't left Delanie. At Sarge's greeting, her gaze rose and connected with his. She blushed, stood straighter, and let her hands fall to her sides.

"I came in early to get fitted with this thing." She patted the protruding bulge over her normally slender waist. "I wasn't sure how long it would take and didn't want you to have to wait."

Eli nodded again, grateful for her thoughtfulness.

Sarge shook some keys, and both Eli and Delanie refocused on the metal ring dangling before them. "An old beat-up Nova. You'll find it out in the fenced lot with the other police vehicles." He tossed the keys to Eli, where he still stood just inside the doorway. "Hit the road."

Eli's gaze returned to Delanie, and he knew Sarge was right. She was the perfect girl for the job. In her black capris, snug-fitting pink maternity T-shirt, and honey-hued locks hanging long and straight, she easily passed as a high school teen. Upon his scrutiny she tugged at the shirt, trying

48

to loosen it across her midsection. "This isn't mine," she assured him. "I don't normally wear things this tight, but they thought I should look the part."

Once again he just nodded and waited for her to exit Sarge's office, then closed the door behind them. On the way out of the building, Delanie received a few wolf whistles and joking remarks from other cops in the hall.

She gave them a sidelong glance. "Grow up, boys." Her gaze returned to him. "Hey, E, I've been doing some checking. My friend Kristen is a paralegal, and she claims Peg's Diner on Sierra Street, just south of downtown, is a favorite hangout for many of Reno's attorneys. Do you want to start there? We can have breakfast, watch who comes and goes, formulate a plan."

Eli gave her a nod, held the door for her, and then led her to the beat-up black car. He opened the passenger door and waited while she struggled with her new protrusion to situate herself in the seat; then he shut the door. Once he turned the key, the engine roared to life.

"Nice pipes."

He glanced at Delanie, surprised she knew anything about mufflers.

She grinned at him. "What—girls can't like souped-up cars?"

He revved the engine. "The mechanics on this car are sure in better shape than the body." He let out the clutch, and they rolled forward toward the gate.

"Well, I'm relieved you don't have laryngitis," Delanie said.

"What?"

"That's the first thing you've said all morning. I thought maybe you'd lost your voice or the cat had your tongue."

Though he hadn't realized it, she was right. Not being one

for idle chitchat, he'd have liked to keep it that way. Delanie, however...

He found a parallel parking spot along the street a couple of blocks from the restaurant. Digging in his pocket, he stuck a few quarters in the meter. Delanie had already exited the car and waited on the sidewalk. Remembering his self-made promise, he grabbed her hand in his, and they sauntered toward Peg's. Her small, warm hand reminded him he hadn't done this hand-holding thing since high school.

"Two, please," he informed Rosie, the hostess, as soon as they entered the building. He noted her curiosity as she gawked at Delanie's pregnant form. She led them to a small booth, and Eli didn't release his clasp on Delanie's hand until they arrived at their destination. Sliding into the seat proved difficult for Delanie. Her belly barely fit.

"You guys lucked out and just missed a big rush." Rosie handed each of them a menu. She directed her next comment at him. "You're running late today. The waitress will be around soon." She turned and walked away.

Delanie's forehead crinkled. "You're a regular here?"

Eli nodded, laid his menu aside, and flipped over the upside-down coffee cup. He was sure she'd have said more, but Sue ambled by just then with a pot in her hand and filled his cup with the rich, dark brew.

"Any for you?" she asked Delanie.

Laying her menu down, Delanie stroked her girth. "It's not good for the baby."

The waitress nodded and moved on.

Delanie checked out the restaurant. Eli had already noted several business professionals but saw no pregnant women dining with any of them.

"This is a fun place—all the colorful pictures on the walls,"

Delanie said with her normal enthusiasm.

Eli perused the light blue walls and shrugged. He'd never paid much attention before.

Another waitress took their orders, grabbing the menus as she left the table.

"You're really a gentleman at heart." Delanie squeezed lemon into her water.

He stared at her. Where had that come from?

"You open building doors and car doors. Not many men are that attentive these days. It's sweet."

Sweet? "My dad always did that for my mom." *Even in a drunken stupor.* "Comes second nature."

"You never speak of your family."

"Nope." *And I never will.*

Sue came by and refilled his cup. "It's good to finally see you here with someone." She smiled at Delanie. "We'd convinced ourselves the man was a hermit."

Delanie returned her smile and rubbed her tummy. "No. He's got me and the baby."

"Good for you," she said and winked at Eli.

"So you don't bring your women here?" Delanie whispered.

He shook his head. *Always fishing.*

"I've never been to this diner before," Delanie said, her gaze roving. Then she focused on him. "Are you married?"

"Nope."

"Me either."

As if he cared.

"Ever been?"

He stared into those tranquil eyes and debated answering. *Might as well. She probably won't let up until I do.* "Nope."

"Me neither."

The waitress set his usual in front of him and a spinach

omelet in front of Delanie. She scrunched her nose at his *huevos rancheros*. "How can you eat that this early in the morning?"

"How can you talk so much this early in the morning?" he countered.

She grinned, apparently undaunted by his intended dig. Sometimes her beauty nearly stole his breath. Her skin glowed with peaches-and-cream perfection. The kiss from yesterday floated to the forefront of his mind, and he wanted to repeat it. No wonder he steered clear of all women; he obviously had no willpower whatsoever. Clearing his throat, he hoped to clear his thoughts, as well.

"My brother sometimes orders the same Mexican egg dish, but yours looks different." She pointed at his plate with her fork.

"It's served in a tortilla."

"And smothered in hot sauce," she noted.

Eli decided that since peace and quiet didn't appear to be an option, they might as well at least discuss work—a safer topic than his personal life. "I think I might have gotten a lead last night."

Delanie laid down her fork and leaned forward.

"I was at the Burger House up by where I live." She nodded, and he recounted the incident. "I had hoped to see them climb into a car so I could ID the vehicle, but they were nowhere to be seen. I searched both sides of the parking lot. The guys thought the girl went to their middle school a couple of years ago. Said she was in eighth when they were in sixth grade, so that would probably make her a sophomore. I thought I could get the police artist to sketch both her and the man with her. Might be our first lead."

Delanie chewed her lower lip, appearing deep in thought.

"We could search all of the local attorney Web sites and see if we can find a picture that matches."

"Good plan. I also thought we'd visit Clayton Middle School and see if the principal or anyone else recognizes the girl."

"Okay." Delanie pushed away more than half of her breakfast. "I think I'll ditch this huge obstruction"—she looked down—"and put on my jeans. I don't know how women manage this."

Sue refilled Eli's coffee a third time. "You didn't like your omelet, honey?"

"No, it was delicious—just too much."

"You're eating for two now. You'd better pick it up a notch," she warned and cleared Delanie's plate. "And you—you never leave a scrap behind." She grabbed Eli's empty plate.

"How often do you come here?" Delanie asked, crawling out of the booth. He offered her a hand and pulled her to her feet.

"Hey, you never get up and fix me breakfast." Eli grabbed the check. "A man's got to eat."

Delanie's cheeks turned a pink shade. He wrapped his arm around her and nuzzled her ear while Rosie rang up their ticket. She eyed Delanie over her bifocals. "You'd best feed your man, honey. Otherwise somebody else will. Just ask my ex."

"Thanks. I'll remember that." Delanie glanced at him.

He leaned in and kissed her—slow, soft, sweet.

"Ahem." The hostess got their attention and held out Eli's change.

He grabbed Delanie's hand and led her out the door. Halfway to the car Eli said, "I finally figured out how to shut you up."

Delanie tugged on his arm and stopped. She faced him. "About that." Her voice was quiet and breathless.

He dropped her hand and lifted his to her cheek; cupping her face he kissed her again. Her arms slipped around his neck and his around her back. He drew her closer—as close as her newly acquired tummy would allow. He convinced himself he was only doing this to bug her—nothing in him actually wanted to kiss her. Nope—nothing at all.

"Stop!" She ran her fingers over her lips as if to erase the moment. "This isn't right. We can look like a couple without making out right here for all the world to see."

Eli grinned. He'd gotten to her. "I'm just following orders," he said innocently. Maybe she'd request another partner—he could only hope.

"I'll talk to Joe if I need to, but I don't think this assignment has to go against my religious convictions."

Eli chose to taunt her. "Don't tell me you're one of those virgins who wants her first kiss to happen at the altar. Too late for that now, baby."

Delanie put her hands on her hips. "For your information, I have kissed guys before. But what is wrong with being a virgin? In other societies it was considered a virtue, but in twenty-first-century America, it's looked down on. Why?"

Eli gave her his usual shrug. He honestly admired her for going against the grain, but of course he wouldn't tell her that. Someday some fortunate guy would be her first and only. Good for her. Lucky him.

⠂⠁

Delanie crossed her arms over her padded stomach. "I'm sorry you feel like my convictions are a joke. It's important to me, so if you can't refrain from kissing me—"

"Let me assure you, Delanie Cooper—you're not that hard to resist." He tilted his head in that cocky way of his. "I can refrain. Believe me, I can refrain."

His words verified what she'd thought all along. He found her repulsive, and the silly thing was, that fact bothered her. Swallowing hard, she asked, "Then will you?"

"No problem. You tell me where your lines are, and I won't cross them." Eli started moving toward the car.

"Fair enough." She outlined her boundaries—"Arm around my shoulder, holding hands, and maybe an occasional hug. Nothing more."

"Fine." He opened her car door.

"Good." Delanie relaxed, relieved to have that conversation over but also a little saddened by their spat. Would they ever be able to discuss things without childish quarrels?

They drove back to the police station in silence. While Eli met with the artist and worked on the sketches, Delanie ditched her belly and the maternity wear, then searched the Web and phone book for local attorneys fitting the description Eli provided. Not all lawyers had their pictures posted, so she knew her chances were slim. Someone into illegal activity normally didn't want his face plastered all over the Internet or yellow pages.

Eli joined her at the computer. "Any luck?"

She shook her head, taking the sketches he held out. "No, there was no one who resembled this guy." Then she studied the young girl's face. "She's so young."

"Too young to be a mom—that's for sure." Eli's shoulders slumped, and Delanie understood his burden for these young girls. "Before we head over to the middle school," Eli continued, "we should go for the hard-to-identify look—you know, hats and sunglasses. If you could stuff your hair in a cap. The more nondescript we are, the better."

Opening a locker, he handed Delanie a cap and grabbed one for himself.

"The Angels, huh?" She worked at stuffing her shoulder-length hair up into the cap. "Your favorite team?"

"Yep. Let's do it."

Delanie grabbed her sunglasses from her purse and an empty file folder from the file cabinet. She slipped the drawings inside. "Ready to roll."

Arriving at Clayton Middle, they followed signs to the office. "We'd like to see the principal, please," Eli requested.

"Do you have an appointment?" the secretary asked from her desk, not even coming to the counter where they stood.

"No, I'm sorry. We don't."

"But it *is* most important," Delanie tacked on.

Mrs. Simmons—as her name placard identified her—gawked at them over her bifocals. "Mr. McNally is a busy man." She refocused on her computer, typed a few keystrokes, and informed them, "He can see you a week from Friday."

Delanie glanced at Eli. He gave her an almost imperceptible nod. A thrill surged through her; she realized they'd made their first connection as partners. Simultaneously they both pulled out their badges.

"I think now is better," Eli told the staunch, follow-the-rules woman.

Her eyes grew large. "Yes, sir." She disappeared behind a door but returned quickly to summon them in.

Eli made the introductions, and they both shook the balding Mr. McNally's hand. "What can I do for you today?"

Delanie pulled out the sketch.

"We wondered if you could identify this young girl," Eli said. "A witness believes she attended school here a couple of years ago."

The principal took the sketch, studied it, and hit the button on the intercom perched on his desk.

"Yes, sir?" The voice of Mrs. Simmons echoed into the room.

"Hilda, could you come in here a moment?"

"Certainly, sir." In a matter of seconds, the school secretary entered the office.

Mr. McNally held up the sketch. "Isn't this that. . . ?" He snapped his fingers, searching for a name. "Anderson, Alden—"

"I think it might be Brandi Alexander, sir. She's in high school now."

"Thank you, Hilda." He dismissed her with a wave of his hand.

"One moment." Delanie guessed the woman might be more likely to know the answer to her next question. She pulled out the second pencil drawing. "Is this her father?" She held it up so they could see.

They both moved in closer to study the picture. The principal shook his head. "I don't believe I've ever seen this man before." He glanced to Mrs. Simmons. "You?"

"No, and I don't think Brandi had a dad that was around. So many of the kids don't. I can't be sure, but I don't recall one."

Mr. McNally placed a call to the high school Brandi would have transferred to. He covered the mouthpiece with his hand and whispered, "She's enrolled there. Would you like me to let them know you're on the way?"

"Sure." Eli held the door open for Delanie. "And thank you."

They rushed to the car, Delanie's heart pounding with the anticipation of making headway in the case. This was when she loved being a cop the most, when the pieces of the puzzle started coming together. Would the case end today, and would Eli be out of her life so soon?

six

"Well, so far this afternoon is a bust," Delanie said as they drove away from Brandi's neighborhood.

"Not completely," Eli corrected.

"Excuse me. Are you being optimistic?" She couldn't resist the jab.

"Never," he assured her. "But even though Brandi wasn't in school today, we know she's enrolled."

"Yeah, but she hasn't been there for the past two weeks."

"True, but we've got her address, and even though no one was home, we know where she lives," Eli reminded Delanie. "Plus the school secretary slipped us the address without forcing us to take the extra time to obtain a warrant."

"You're right." Delanie shifted in her seat, not missing her round belly one bit. "I just was so ready to solve the case today."

Eli chuckled. "You thought we'd go to the high school, interview her, she'd spill the beans, and we'd go make the arrest?"

Delanie rolled her eyes. "Not quite that cut-and-dried, but, yes, I'd hoped we'd be well on our way to closing this case." She stretched her neck, loosening a kink. "Where are we going now?" she asked when Eli turned in the opposite direction from the department.

"Thought we'd go hang out at that Burger House for a while—see who we might see." He glanced at her. "How long have you been a plainclothes detective?"

"Since Monday," Delanie said weakly. She studied the passing scenery, not wishing to witness Eli's reaction.

"Well then, you have a lot to learn. I'm guessing this case will take us at least three months, if not more."

She'd mentally prepared for him to mock her because this was her first undercover assignment, so she was surprised when he didn't. "You're kidding? Three months?" Even though she hated the fact that she became so angry yesterday, her little outburst must have paid off.

He shook his head, turning into the restaurant's parking lot. "Once we figure out who the culprit is, it could take months to flush them out. When people are making a lot of money doing illegal activity, they know how to cover their tracks."

Eli cut the engine. Once inside they ordered a late lunch, and then he led her straight to a table in the back corner. It was actually a large booth with a wraparound seat. "This way we can each see the doors and who uses them." He slid in until his back faced the front window of the building. She slid in the opposite side and sat at a ninety-degree angle to him.

"Amazing how much easier it is to occupy a booth without that big belly." Delanie laughed.

Eli jabbed his straw into his cup and took a long sip. "We can go over today's discoveries, and I also thought we should review the police report Julie Johnson's mom filed." Eli ran his hand through his dark hair.

"Sounds like a plan," Delanie agreed, unwrapping her fish sandwich. Eli certainly was talkative when the topic was work and not personal. Maybe she could slide in a few personal inquiries in the midst of their case conversation.

After taking a bite of his burger, Eli pulled a legal pad from his backpack and made three columns. At the top he labeled them KNOW, SUSPECT, and To Do. "What do we know for sure?"

Delanie set her cup down. "Julie Johnson is dead."

"Brandi is pregnant," Eli added. He jotted the facts in a scribbled form Delanie wondered if she could ever decipher. "She has a single mom and no siblings."

"Her neighbor believes she plans to give the baby up for adoption."

"I'll put that under 'SUSPECT' because we didn't hear it from Brandi herself." They continued recalling info and categorizing it as they finished lunch.

One of the restaurant employees was cleaning the tables after the lunch rush. She stopped at their table. "I've never seen you in here without them boys before." Though she spoke to Eli, her gaze never left Delanie, inquisitiveness written all over her face. She moved on to the table next to theirs and cleared the trash.

"You must come in here often." Delanie kept her voice low.

"Couple of times a week. You've heard the way to a man's heart is through his stomach?"

Delanie nodded.

"Junior high boys aren't any different. I feed them in hopes of gaining their loyalty."

"Loyalty?" Delanie thought the statement seemed odd.

Eli wadded up the wrapper from his burger. "If they feel loyalty to me and to our little group, feel like they have a place to belong, they'll be less likely to join a gang. Everybody needs a sense of belonging, a sense of fitting in and importance. We all need to know there are people who care."

Delanie wondered what people Eli had. "So in a sense, you've become family to those boys."

Eli nodded. "And them to each other. Sadly, most come

from single-parent families where their mom or dad is working long hours, sometimes two jobs, just to put food on the table. They don't have much left to invest in their kids."

Eli, you're a good man. "So you do it for them?"

"Not in place of, but I try to come alongside the parents."

"Why?"

He shrugged. "Why not?"

"Don't get me wrong. I think what you're doing is wonderful. I'm involved in a youth program—Cops-N-Kidz. Maybe you've heard of it?"

Eli nodded.

"It's a joint venture between my church and Cops for Christ. A big warehouse downtown was donated to us, so we've refurbished it and made a cool place for kids to hang. You're welcome to bring your crew by anytime."

"I don't think so. We're pretty busy." He blew off her invitation.

She studied his blue-green eyes that changed with his mood and what he wore. Today his navy T-shirt made them look totally blue, not a speck of green to be found.

"So what keeps you guys busy?" She tried to sound off-handed, uninterested, but she still wanted more information on this enigma of a man.

"How did this conversation get to be about me?" he asked.

Delanie shrugged. Even though he'd deny it, she sensed a change in Eli. "Just curious about your little gang and how you come alongside the parents. At CNK we rarely see a parent, and I'd like to change that. Thought you could offer some suggestions."

"Still Coop the Snoop, I see." He made the statement with a slight grin, though, so she pushed for more information.

"For a good cause," she reminded him. "How did you get

started in this endeavor? Was it hard to gain the parents' trust?"

Eli didn't jump right in with answers but pondered her questions. He studied her earnest expression. Her petite appearance camouflaged a much tougher woman than people would guess. He'd learned that lesson and wouldn't forget anytime soon.

As he debated how much to share, weariness settled over him. He was sick of dodging the truth, hiding the ugliness of his past, and closing up to anyone interested enough to ask. Delanie's openness caused him to wish for the same freedom.

"I grew up much the way they are. My mother left when I was twelve, so it was just my old man and me. He was a functioning alcoholic. Now he's no longer functioning— spends his days in an alcoholic haze. Anyway, often days would go by, and I'd never see him. He'd leave for work before I was up and stumble in long after I'd hit the sack. It was a lonely existence. So when my dad and I moved into the complex seven years ago and I saw all these young boys with the same kind of life I'd known, I decided to invest."

Compassion filled Delanie's expression, not pity. He appreciated that. Her crescent eyes shone with admiration, and that was enough to keep his story rolling. He'd never had a woman gaze at him with the respect he saw on her face. Man, did that make him feel ten feet tall.

"I resolved to fill whatever gaps I could in these kids' lives. I'm their friend, their greatest fan, and their teacher. I tutor them twice a week, take them to games at the college—"

"Feed them burgers, shoot hoops with them. Sounds like you do all the things my dad did for us."

A pang of longing hit him. "Then you were a lucky little girl." Her childhood contrasted starkly with his.

"I was." Her expression reflected a contentment he'd never known. "But how do you do it? I don't even think I could remember junior high math, let alone teach someone else."

"I couldn't either—had to take a couple of refresher courses at the junior college in order to bring my long-forgotten skills up to speed."

"You did that? Just for them?" She'd tipped her head to the side a bit, and her voice rang with approval, as if he'd made the greatest sacrifice of all time. "You're the most giving person I've ever known."

Her smile reached all the way to her eyes and all the way to his heart—it danced to her praise. He'd never received many accolades and had to admit it was nice.

"Maybe my motives are selfish. All I know is I'm determined to do everything in my power to keep these boys in school, out of gangs, and off drugs. It's their only hope for a halfway decent life. My deepest desire is for them to graduate from high school and make something of their lives."

"They have a much better chance with you involved."

Eli smiled. He'd never shared those thoughts with another living soul. Something about her made a man want to be better than he was, do more than he thought he could. *I'm falling for her.* The realization scared the socks off him. Nothing could come of the unfortunate boy from the wrong side of town and the chief's daughter. Besides, he was a lifelong, card-carrying member of the "I'll be single forever" club. *Time for us to get back on track. Time for me to get back on track and remember my plans and goals. No women, not now, not ever—too much pain, too little return.*

"We have work to do." He rummaged through his backpack and dug out the copy of the report filed by Mrs. Johnson. Delanie followed suit.

"Julie Johnson was reported as a runaway in April." He read the file in a low tone. "Four months later, in August, she placed a call to her mother. During the conversation she revealed being eight months' pregnant. Last week her body was discovered, and the autopsy revealed she'd given birth hours before someone strangled her and placed her in a shallow grave not too far east of town." He paused, taking a deep breath. "I never thought I'd say this, but in many ways this assignment is more tragic than the drug unit." His gaze locked with Delanie's. "There I dealt with criminal masterminds selling drugs but wasn't face-to-face with death. I mean, murder happens, people OD—but my main job was just to set people up, bust them, and ship them to prison." He shook his head and knew he'd never get over this young girl losing her life because a greedy person sold the child she carried inside. Human trafficking.

Delanie squeezed his hand. "That's why we're cops, right?" She picked up the report. "Here are the bits of conversation Mrs. Johnson remembers." Delanie started reading. "When she answered her phone in the middle of the afternoon, her daughter said, 'Mom, I'm sorry.' Mrs. Johnson remembers the relief that washed over her, knowing Julie was alive. She asked if her daughter was okay. Julie was hard to understand because she was not only crying but also talking very fast and very soft. Her mother struggled to distinguish her actual words." Delanie took a sip of her diet soda.

Eli continued. "Julie said she was eight months' pregnant and had been offered a lot of money for her baby, which of course sounded wonderful to a thirteen-year-old girl. After feeling the baby move and grow inside of her, she'd changed her mind. Mrs. Johnson asked where she was and who was going to give her the money. She thought Julie said 'the doctor' but didn't name a specific person. Suddenly she heard Julie scream, some muffled wrestling-type sounds, and the phone went dead. Mrs. Johnson has caller ID, but the call came from a private name, private number. She immediately called the police in hysterics; they were able to have the call traced, but it came from a prepaid cell phone."

"Every end is a dead end." Delanie rested her face in her hands. "A young girl wondering if she was pregnant wouldn't go to a doctor."

"You're right," Eli agreed. "She'd go to the corner drugstore, buy a pregnancy test, and find out for herself."

Delanie nodded. "Exactly."

"There has to be a source enlightening young pregnant girls about earning a lot of money by having their baby. I mean, if they're already pregnant, why not?"

"Turns a negative into a positive, or so it would seem."

"We've got the bait." Eli focused on Delanie. "At least when you're wearing your disguise."

"Now we just need someone to bite."

"Our hope is that Brandi will." He pictured the young teen he'd seen in this very spot just the night before.

"If we can find her."

"Why don't I pay a visit to her house about 7:00 a.m. tomorrow? Maybe at that time both she and her mom will be home." Eli started repacking his strewn paperwork into an unzipped pocket on his backpack. "You can wait in the car so she doesn't see you. I'll be wired, and you'll hear everything. Then if the direct approach doesn't work, we'll plant you in her path as plan B."

"Why risk the direct approach? Why not start with me?"

He slid out of the booth. "Plan B can take weeks, if not months." He watched her gather her things. "It takes time to build a relationship and glean information, but sometimes the up-front method can reap immediate results." He automatically offered his hand as she slipped out from her side of the table. Something had changed between them this afternoon, and try as he might, he hadn't been able to resist opening up to her.

She glanced at the plain watch wrapped around her slender wrist. "My dogs are going to hate you for disrupting their run."

"Dogs, huh?"

"Hank and Junie." On the drive back to the station, she filled him in on their antics and their need for a daily jog.

When he dropped her off at her car, he said, "Give Hank and Junie my apologies."

She turned slightly in her seat to face him. "I will."

The air crackled between them. He had a sudden urge to kiss her. Her eyes told him she had the same urge. He cleared his throat. "Well, see ya."

"Yeah, first thing in the morning."

He waited until she was safely in her car before driving the Nova back into the fenced lot.

You're taking care of her, a little voice in his head accused. "Shut up."

seven

At Delanie's request Eli parked as close as possible to the Alexander home without the car actually being in clear view of the windows and doors. They were about five doors down and across the street. Her stomach knotted, thinking about sending her partner out alone with little to no backup. She wondered if she'd feel apprehensive with just any old partner or if she felt this way because it was Eli—the man who'd already become dear to her. The guy she prayed for night and day.

"Eli?"

"Huh?" He didn't look up but reholstered his gun. He'd finished checking the chamber.

"Be careful." Was that her voice, fearful and apprehensive? She knew she was overreacting and being silly but couldn't help herself.

He glanced in her direction. "I will. I'm wired for sound, so you'll know everything that's going down. Plus with these"—he held up the binoculars—"you can see pretty well."

Against her better judgment, she reached out and squeezed his hand. "I'll be praying."

Handing her the binoculars, he said, "You do that." Sending her a crooked smile, he was on his way. She focused the binoculars and watched him walk to the third house and cross the street.

The neighborhood was run-down—trash in front yards, old cars with parts lying loose on the ground surrounding them, and weeds growing knee-high. When she heard Eli's knock on the front door, her heart doubled its speed. She focused on Eli.

"Lord," she whispered, "give us wisdom and keep us safe, especially Eli."

"Whoa!" Delanie reacted to the scantily clad woman who opened the door; her audacity surprised Delanie.

"Hello there. What can I do for you?" The woman's voice purred, and even from where the car was parked, Delanie could tell her body language was flirtatious. Jealousy pounced on her like a mountain lion on its prey.

"Are you Mrs. Alexander?" Eli's voice was no-nonsense, and relief washed over Delanie.

"Honey, I haven't been Mrs. Anybody in years. The better question, who are you?"

Eli pulled out his badge. "Eli Logan. I'm a detective with Reno PD. I'm actually here to see your daughter, Brandi."

"Oh man, what's she done now? Not more shoplifting. Brandi, you get down here right now!" She screamed so loudly the sound hurt Delanie's ear.

The mother, whatever her name was, disappeared into the house. Eli waited on the porch. A few minutes later Brandi was shoved out the door. She wore a knit tank top that no longer covered her protruding belly or met her plaid pajama bottoms. With eyes barely open she said, "I didn't do anything."

"I'm not here because you did," Eli assured her. "I wanted to talk to you about your baby."

Even through the binoculars Delanie saw a mask slip over Brandi's face, and her expression went from sleepy to alert and guarded. Brandi laid her arm and hand across the unborn child. "What about my baby?"

"I understand the child is up for adoption."

Her eyes squinted against the rising sun. "No. You heard wrong."

"I'm not feeding another mouth. I already told you that!" Though Delanie couldn't see Brandi's mother, she must have been just inside the front door.

Brandi swung around. "Everything is taken care of."

"How is everything taken care of?" Eli asked.

Brandi faced him, arms folded over her chest. "I haven't done anything illegal, so I don't think it's any of your business."

"Baby selling is illegal."

She glared at Eli but made no response.

"You are selling the baby, right?"

She made a little snorting noise. "I am not selling my baby. For your information, a nice couple is adopting it."

"Are you being financially compensated in any way?" Eli's voice was compassionate and caring, not harsh and demanding as some cops often were. Every day he moved a little deeper into her heart, and Delanie knew she wouldn't leave this case unscathed.

Brandi fidgeted with the drawstring on her PJs, ignoring Eli.

"If you're getting money for that baby, I'd better know about it." Her mom was yelling again.

This poor kid had no one on her team who cared about her. She'd be easy prey for any compassionate person, even just a doctor and a lawyer pretending to be compassionate. She might not be savvy enough to know they weren't really on her team.

"Brandi, just give me a name, and you'll never see me again."

"George." Her tone was laced with sarcasm. "The baby's name is George." She turned to go back into the house.

"Wait." He grabbed her arm to stop her forward movement. "Another girl, even younger than you, was murdered just after the birth of her baby. These are not nice people."

She glared at the hand holding her arm.

Eli released her, and she disappeared into the house. He handed her mother his card, though all Delanie could see was her arm. "This is serious, not to mention illegal. Please talk to her and call me. All I need is the name of the doctor or lawyer she's dealing with."

The door shut, and Eli let out a long, deep breath. His head drooped, and several seconds later he turned and moved toward the car. She wished she could comfort him but knew she must keep her distance, so neither spoke when he hopped into the car.

They drove to the police station, and Delanie followed Eli to Joe's office. He rapped once on the half-closed door, and Joe hollered, "Yeah?"

Eli pushed the door open and stood back to let Delanie enter first. They each plopped into a green vinyl chair.

"What's up?" Joe pushed aside his paperwork and focused on them.

They reviewed the case notes with him, and Delanie asked both men, "So what's next?"

"Let's put a twenty-four-hour tail on her for the next couple of weeks. Can you guys cover twelve?"

Eli nodded.

Delanie hesitated. *There goes my life. I'll have to see if Hank and Junie can stay at Mom and Dad's during the day.*

"Delanie?" Joe raised his brows.

"Sure." Though she felt far from sure. She and Eli together twelve hours a day, seven days a week, crammed into a car for most of it, held zero appeal.

"Which twelve do you want?" Joe asked, his gaze flitting from one to the other.

"Nine to nine—the daylight shift," Eli answered.

There go evenings.

"That okay with you, Delanie?" Joe focused his full attention on her.

"I was hoping more like six to six. That way we'd still have our evenings."

Joe's gaze returned to Eli.

"The reason I thought nine is because the girl was still sound asleep at seven this morning. We'd be sitting for several hours doing nothing. Plus I'd like to get a pulse on her evening activity."

"All good points. Delanie, why six?" Joe asked.

"The youth center. I'm scheduled there three evenings a week."

Eli gave her a pointed stare. "Maybe your life is better suited for the regular hours a patrol car provides."

"Still hoping to rid yourself of me?" She returned his look with one just as pointed, then looked at Joe. "Nine to nine will be fine." She smiled sweetly at Eli. *You're not winning that easily.*

"Why don't you both take the rest of today off? We'll start the stakeout at nine tomorrow morning. I'm going to issue you a different car in case they spotted the Nova. Eli, if you want to hang around, I'll send you home with it today. Then you can just pick up Delanie each morning and drop her at the end of the day. Save you both the extra time of coming here."

Delanie wrote out the directions to her place for Eli before she left. Eli said he'd turn in the equipment they'd used today.

What do I do with a day off in the middle of the week? Delanie exited the police station and headed for her car. Feeling restless and needing to process everything going on inside her, she glanced at her watch. Barely midmorning. Jodi would be tied up with her first graders for several more hours. Courtney was pulling a twelve-hour shift at the hospital. Kristen might be able to catch an early lunch. She pushed the number 8 on her cell phone, and the call went to Kristen's cell.

"Hey, D, you don't normally call me in the middle of the day. Everything okay?"

"You want to grab an early lunch? I'm free for the rest of the day, and then life as I know it will end for two weeks."

"That sounds like enough enticement to get me to drop everything. Where?"

"Where else?"

Kristen laughed. "Bertha's. I'll be there in about ten minutes."

Delanie decided to walk, clear her head, and grab some fresh air. She'd probably get there about the same time as Kristen.

The host led her to a small booth with a red tablecloth and brown vinyl seats. She faced the lone rock wall inside the place. All of the others were wood paneled. Kristen joined her. Neither even bothered with the menus. They both ordered their old standbys and would share.

"So what's up, girlfriend, and why are you disappearing for two weeks?" One of Kristen's arched brows rose.

"Eli and I will be doing surveillance for the next fourteen days—nine to nine."

"There goes your life."

"Yep, and possibly my sanity." Delanie sipped her iced tea the waiter had just dropped off.

"Sanity?" Kristen's brow wrinkled.

"I cannot tell you how attracted I am to this man. I think I'm falling in love with him. I mean, is that even possible in such a short amount of time?"

"You're asking the wrong girl. I'm still waiting, so I don't even know what falling feels like."

"Me either, having never done it myself, but he is always popping up in my thoughts."

"Always on my mind—sounds like a country western song my dad used to like." Then she proceeded to sing the chorus.

Kristen could always make her laugh. "He is always on my mind. I fall asleep praying for him. I wake up thinking about him. When he smiles, my heart does this little flutter thing."

"You sure it's not a heart attack?" Kristen quipped.

The waiter delivered their food, and they did their usual swapping. After praying, Kristen said, "I'm sorry, D. I know this is hard for you, but laughter is good medicine. I'll be good. Pinkie promise." She held up her pinkie like they did as kids. "Finish your story."

"He's just this incredible guy with character and integrity and everything I'd want in a man—everything except Christ. Sad to say, but he's better than most Christian guys."

Kristen's face showed concern. "What are you going to do?"

"Nothing. What can I do?" She took a bite of her taco. "But for the first time in my life, I understand how easy it would be to fall for an unbeliever. I've always been all smug, thinking it could never happen to me. But it could. It is."

"I guess it's not whether it happens, but what you do when it happens that matters." Kristen's eyes held compassion, and her words held truth.

"Yeah. I'm learning it's easy to have the answers until the rubber of life meets the road of faith. Anyway, pray that I'll stand firm. Some days I just want to chuck all my ideals and grab hold of life, but I know in the long run the cost would be too high. I don't want to rob myself of God's best." Delanie sighed. "Enough about me. How are you?"

"I'm fine. Status quo and all."

"I'll miss not seeing you guys at the youth center, at church, at Bible study."

"It'll be weird, that's for sure."

"I'm also worried about all that intense time with Eli, so don't forget to pray for me."

"I will. Every day." She held up her pinkie again. "Promise." They both chuckled.

"I have another favor. . . ."

Kristen glanced up from her food.

"Can you get me a list of lawyers who do adoptions?"

Kristen nodded. "Sure—no problem."

"Can you also do a little fishing? See if any of the partners in your firm have heard of anyone arranging—shall we say—some very high-priced adoptions."

"Ooh, intrigue, mystery—I love it. I'll see what I can find."

"Discreetly." Delanie felt the need to tack that on.

"Are you saying I lack discretion?" Kristen feigned a hurt expression.

"You're funny, you're direct, but sometimes. . ."

"I know, I know—a bull in a china shop. I've heard that one before." Kristen wasn't afraid to laugh at herself either— a great quality.

"One more request," Delanie said while searching through her wallet for a tip. "This is really out there, but can you make me a list of all the attorneys with George in their names? First, last, middle—doesn't matter."

"George, huh?" Kristen frowned and shrugged. "Okay."

"Unless you come across pertinent info, I'll just get all

this from you when my two weeks of torture end." Delanie laughed and slipped from the booth. "We won't be checking out attorneys until then."

After paying their bills, they hugged and said their good-byes.

❧

Eli suffered through being in Delanie's presence day in and day out. She'd been quiet and withdrawn—said very little and asked no questions. He wasn't sure which was worse—the energetic, talkative Delanie or this one. He was thankful their two weeks were almost over. One more day after today. The whole stakeout had been a complete waste of time.

The kid was a couch potato to the max. They'd tailed her to the mall a couple of times, but other than that, she watched TV and played video games. He knew that from the bug Sarge had planted. He'd obtained a warrant, and while Delanie and Eli trailed Brandi last week, Sarge sent a crew in to do the job.

Today was no different. Here they sat watching, waiting, bored to tears. He missed his junior high brood. This assignment certainly wasn't worth giving up his time with them.

At Sarge's request Delanie had worn her pregnant teen getup the last couple of days, in case Brandi hit the mall again. Delanie didn't complain, but he knew from watching her that the bulky thing was uncomfortable and probably hot.

She'd laid her seat back and grabbed a few minutes of shut-eye. They took turns with the afternoon siesta. For a little thing, she was tough as nails. She'd earned his respect in so many ways, but most of all for her performance as a cop. And she read him like a book. He hadn't had a partner he'd been this in sync with since Gus, and that was more than five years ago.

She opened her eyes and caught him gawking. When she smiled up at him, he nearly forgot to breathe.

"Welcome back to the wonderful and exciting life of an undercover cop." He had to say something, or they would have gaped at each other forever. Sometimes when he stared into her eyes, he was certain she was crazy about him, but her actions never supported his theory. Not that he cared anyway. Things were better off this way.

She pulled the lever on the side of her seat to return it to the upright position. "Who knew what I'd been missing all these years?" she joked. "Eighty-four hours a week in a car. It's like being back on patrol, but we never move."

Eli laughed.

"She's coming out!" Delanie pointed to the house.

"I'll follow on foot. You hang back in the car." Eli raised his pant leg and checked his pistol. "Our wire should work for about a block or two, so you'll have to stay fairly close."

Delanie nodded and went around the car to the driver's seat.

"Be careful and watch your back." Eli closed the car door and started a casual stroll down the street. As he rounded the corner at the end of the block, he heard Delanie start the car and glimpsed her rolling forward. Eli kept his eye on Delanie about a half block back, and Brandi was about the same distance ahead.

As expected, Brandi led them to the mall. Eli kept her in sight while Delanie parked the car. He instructed Delanie where to enter the mall so she'd be in Brandi's path. Brandi's first stop was the food court, and Delanie stepped into line right behind her. *This couldn't have worked out better.* Eli settled at a table in the back corner.

"So when are you due?" Delanie asked in a casual tone.

Brandi turned. "You scared me. I didn't know anyone was behind me."

"Sorry." He couldn't see Delanie's face, but he imagined her warm smile winning Brandi's trust. "This is my first baby, and I have a million questions."

"Me, too!" Brandi said.

"Next!" the man behind the counter yelled.

Brandi moved forward and ordered.

"Get her to lunch with you," Eli spoke softly. Delanie gave a slight nod, and he knew her receptor was working.

"Next."

Delanie ended up at the register beside Brandi. "Hey, are you here by yourself?"

"Why?" The one word was riddled with suspicion.

"I just hate to eat alone. Don't worry—I'm not an ax murderer or anything. I just thought if you were here by yourself, too, we could talk about babies and pregnancy and stretch marks." Delanie paid for her order. "It's okay if you don't want to." She raised her left shoulder in a *whatever* gesture.

Brandi picked up the tray with her order on it. "Sure, I guess. I'll grab us a table over that way." She pointed in Eli's direction, and he quickly raised the newspaper he'd carried in—just in case. He couldn't risk her seeing him. She'd flee for sure.

"Her back is toward you," Delanie said softly into her lapel.

He lowered the paper just enough to keep an eye on things. His gaze connected with Delanie's for a brief second as she set her tray on the table. This being her first undercover assignment, she handled herself well, like a pro. She was relaxed and natural. He supposed he shouldn't have been surprised; everything about her was exceptional.

"Do you have stretch marks?" Delanie made a disgusted face, and Eli smiled.

Brandi only nodded.

"Man, I have like two hundred of them." Delanie looked around. "Are you expecting someone?" She crinkled her nose the way she often did when she asked a question.

"No, why?"

Delanie shrugged. "I don't know. Your eyes are darting around like you're searching for someone."

"Good girl!" Eli whispered. "Thanks for the tip. I'll keep my eyes peeled." Delanie had taken a bite of her burger when he started talking. She was a quick thinker. That way she had a natural break in conversation with Brandi and could focus on his words.

"So when are you due?" Delanie asked between mouthfuls.

"I'm not really sure."

Eli wished he could see Brandi's face—easier to read a person.

"So I guess you don't know the sex of the baby, then?"

"I don't really want to talk about babies." She rose. "I gotta go." She left her barely touched lunch behind and rushed from the food court.

Delanie turned to watch Brandi depart. Eli scanned the area, but no one was following Brandi as far as he could tell. "Stay put," he told Delanie. She kept eating as if nothing had happened. He carried his paper casually to the trash. While facing the can, he said, "I'll see if I can find her."

eight

The following morning Delanie tied the laces on her running shoes. She'd started jogging with her dogs before work and then leaving them at her parents' for the day. Twelve hours was too long without a puppy potty break. Her parents had a doggie door, so her pets were free to roam in and out.

"How does someone just disappear?" Delanie asked Hank as she hooked his leash to his collar. They'd lost Brandi, and Joe was not happy. She still hadn't shown up at home when they left at the end of their twelve. Delanie worried about her and prayed for her all night. The girl was afraid. Delanie knew in her gut that someone had threatened Brandi.

"Junie, I'm in no mood to chase you around," Delanie informed the beagle when she dodged Delanie and dove under the bed.

The doorbell rang. Delanie glanced at her watch. Her gut tightened. Nobody came this early with good news. She ran downstairs, checking her peephole before throwing open the door.

"Eli! We're on duty early. . . ." His expression silenced her.

"Mind if I come in?"

She stepped aside, her heart pounding. Closing the front door, she leaned against it for support. "What's wrong?" Fear lodged itself in her throat, and she barely got the words out.

"Brandi's dead."

She buried her face in her hands. "No!" Lifting her head and focusing on Eli, she begged, "Please tell me it's not true.

Please." Tears streamed down her face, and his face grew hazy.

He took a step toward her. Hank growled.

"Hank, settle." At her command he lay next to his mistress, eyes on Eli, ears pointed straight ahead.

Eli pulled her into his arms. She buried her face in his chest and wept for a girl she barely knew; yet it felt very personal. He held her and stroked her hair, offering comfort.

"Is this our fault?" She raised her head and sniffed. "Did we carelessly endanger her just to close a case?"

Eli's eyes glistened. He swallowed hard. "We followed orders, Delanie." Using his thumbs, he wiped the tears from her cheeks, then rested his forehead against hers.

Junie barked, and they both jumped. "We were just about to take our daily jog." Delanie glanced at the dancing beagle. "I think she resents your intrusion."

"Mind if I go with you?" He was in jeans and a T-shirt, but at least he had on his running shoes.

"If you want." Was he or Joe worrying about her safety?

He nodded. "I've got my workout clothes in the car. I usually hit the gym before I pick you up in the mornings. I'll just be a minute."

While he was gathering his clothes, Delanie went into the downstairs powder room and splashed water on her face. Had she made a mistake changing assignments? More important, had she made a mistake approaching Brandi at the mall?

"I don't think I'm cut out for undercover work," she said when Eli reentered her town house.

He sent her a compassionate smile, his eyes bearing sorrow. "Sometimes—like today—I know I'm not." He touched her cheek for a second, then closed the bathroom door.

Delanie caught her breath and rubbed her fingers where

his had just been. *I've got to be careful. He's doubly dangerous when he's nice.* She grabbed Junie and snapped her leash in place. Moments later the four of them were out in the crisp autumn air. Eli tried to take Hank's leash, but the German shepherd wanted no part of that. Junie, however, had no qualms, so he jogged with the little dog running beside him.

Delanie set the pace and led the way. Eli had no problem matching her step for step, and at the end of the five miles, he seemed to barely break a sweat.

"I need to drop the dogs off at my mom's before work," she said, breathing hard. She halted when reality hit her. "We're not on stakeout today, are we?"

"Sarge told us to take the day off since it's Friday, but on Monday he wants us to find the guy responsible for this."

"A three-day weekend? I feel at a loss to know what to do with myself." She stretched her legs while they stood on the corner of her parents' street. "I may have to go sit in my car for a few hours just to survive."

He grinned at her joke, and her stomach flitted and fluttered. He sure was cute when he smiled, even with hair that needed a trim and a face that needed a shave.

"My parents live down this way." She pointed. "My mom's expecting me, so if you want to head back to your car..."

He shrugged. "I'll go with you." He headed in the direction she'd pointed.

Delanie grabbed his arm, pulling him to a stop. "Eli, am I in danger?"

"Sarge doesn't want you to be alone until we know for sure." They started walking again.

"So you're stuck spending your day off babysitting me?"

"Hey, you're the one who wanted to hang, get to know each other better," Eli reminded her. "You finally got your wish."

"I changed my mind," she informed him—half joking, half deadly serious.

"Gee, thanks." He wore a hurt expression.

But she knew just what they'd do; she'd take him to the youth center. Once he saw how great it was, maybe he'd realize it was the perfect place for his guys to hang out. Then they'd all hear the Word taught, even Eli. Could be a win-win situation—at least that was the hope of her heart.

❧

"Here we are." Delanie led him up the hill at the end of the cul-de-sac to a beige two-story with white trim. This was how he'd imagined her growing up—the perfect well-manicured neighborhood with quiet, tree-lined streets. Following the sidewalk up to the front door, Delanie pulled a key off a chain around her neck. She unlocked the door while Hank and Junie did some sort of happy dance; apparently they enjoyed their visits here.

"Mom?" she called.

Her dad came out of his office, just to the left of the front door. He was tall, in good shape, and toted a full head of silver hair. "Morning, honey." He hugged Delanie and kissed her check.

"Detective Logan." He held out his hand, welcoming Eli.

"Chief Cooper." Eli bobbed his head once.

"I heard about the girl who was murdered last night. I'm sorry." His expression held concern. "Any leads?"

"No, sir."

"It's always harder when it's a kid that dies." He shook his head.

"Where's Mom?" Delanie glanced toward the stairs.

"She had an early meeting this morning. I'm on my way out." He again kissed Delanie's cheek and patted Eli's shoulder. "Lock up on your way out."

"Bye," Eli and Delanie said in unison.

While Delanie put the dogs out back, Eli's gaze roamed the great room. It was warm, peaceful, inviting—everything his place wasn't growing up. Another reminder Delanie Cooper was out of his league, which didn't matter, because he wasn't looking anyway, he told himself again.

On the walk back to her house, Delanie wanted to stop at Walden's for a mocha ole, and they decided to grab breakfast. Being with her felt natural, and their conversation was comfortable. Frankly, it caught him by surprise. He asked about her job on the force, what she'd done so far and who her partners had been, and he shared the same information with her.

Eli checked her town house thoroughly before leaving her safely locked inside—doors and windows secure—then he ran home, showered, and changed. Her home was cozy—a lot of plants, a lot of candles, but not too girly. Nothing fluffy or ruffled. Her taste was simple. He liked it. A man could live there contentedly.

What am I thinking? He caught himself again. Entering his apartment, he was hit with dark, drab, and undecorated. He realized that though his place was clean and tidy, he was ready for more of a home. On his way to the shower he checked on his dad. He was still passed out in his bedroom, fully clothed, shoes and all, lying on top of the covers. Eli shook his head, wishing there was a way to save his dad from this life he'd chosen. But Eli had tried numerous times and in numerous ways. As the old saying went, you can lead a horse to water, but you can't make him drink—or stop drinking, as the case may be. Eli threw a light blanket over him and shut the door.

When he picked up Delanie, she told him she had two things she planned to accomplish today. The first, meet her friend Kristen for coffee and information. The second, go by the youth center and do some cleaning. Since he was curious about the youth center, her plans suited him just fine.

They met Kristen at a café near her office and shared a quick cup of coffee. He noticed her scrutinizing him when she thought he wasn't paying attention. *Wonder what Delanie's said about me.* She handed Delanie a manila envelope on her way out, apologizing for the rush, but she was working on a case that went to trial next week.

Delanie perused the information from Kristen while he drove to the center, not far from downtown in a warehouse district. The old brick building didn't look like anything special on the outside, but the inside impressed him—it was definitely teen-friendly.

"Want a tour?" Delanie asked.

"Sure."

She flipped on the lights. The high small windows kept the building only dimly lit. Now it was bright, and Eli marveled at all they'd done. "This is quite the place." The walls were painted in loud primary colors, and they'd clustered areas together, giving a warm sense rather than a large warehouse feel.

Delanie smiled. "All done with many loving donations and tons of hard work. You should hear the noise level in the evenings and on weekends."

His gaze traversed the huge room. "I bet."

"Except for the kitchen, bathrooms, library, and movie room, everything is in this main area. We figured without walls it would be easier to keep an eye on everything going on."

The entrance was at the center of the building's facade. Off to his left were a couple of pool tables, foosball, Ping-Pong, and several dartboards. "Impressive." Delanie led him to the right, past several couches set in groupings with chairs and love seats surrounding TVs.

"Those are for video games. We closely monitor the games and are selective with what they can play. Now several companies are producing Christian versions of video games, which makes us even happier."

"So everything was donated? It's really pretty nice stuff."

"I know. Isn't it great? A lot of retailers got on board and gave us brand-new stuff. It was so much more than we imagined or hoped for. We sort of expected outdated electronic equipment and old, worn-out plaid couches."

"And what's wrong with worn plaid couches?" Eli joked. "You could be describing my place."

"Nothing is wrong with them," she assured him. "We gladly would have accepted anything and been thrilled to receive it, but my point was, God always gives so much more."

They'd been working together almost a month, and this was her first mention of God. Eli had expected it long before now. "And sometimes He gives so much less."

"What do you mean?" Though she attempted to sound nonchalant, the shocked expression she wore spoke volumes.

"He doesn't come through for everybody. That's all I'm saying."

Delanie paused and seemed to choose her words with care. "Maybe it looks that way—"

"No, Delanie, it *is* that way."

❧

Her heart actually hurt as he slung unfounded accusations of her loving heavenly Father. She sent up a quick prayer, asking God to heal his hurt and disillusionment. Should she argue God's cause or simply agree to disagree? "I'm sorry you feel that way, but if you'd just get to know Him, you'd discover He's a good and loving God."

"How good is a God who ignores the pleas of a twelve-year-old boy, begging for his brother's life? How good is a God who allows that same kid's mother to leave the day after his brother's funeral? How good is a God who lets some doctor cut open a fifteen-year-old girl, steal her baby, and leave her in a back alley to bleed to death?" His jaw and fists were clenched, and his eyes glistened with tears he seemed determined to keep at bay. And his intense pain became hers.

This morning he'd comforted her, and this afternoon her prayer was to do the same for him. She wrapped her arms around his waist and laid her head against his chest. "I'm sorry, Eli. So sorry." At first he remained stiff, arms at his side, but finally he hugged her back. His silent tears ran down his face, and she felt them drop onto her head.

I love this man, and he hates my Lord. Delanie wept for him, for Brandi, and for the "them" that could never be. Eli held her for a long time.

When Eli took her home late that evening, he rechecked her apartment. On his way out the door, he kissed her cheek. "Thanks for everything. See ya Monday."

Locking the door behind him, she wondered what he'd thought of the youth center as it filled up with teens earlier this evening. He'd shot pool with some of the guys and even listened attentively when a couple of ex–gang members shared their testimonies. She prayed for a seed to be planted.

❧

Eli planned to spend his entire Saturday with his junior high buddies. It had been two long weeks since they'd had more than fifteen minutes together. When he awoke to the sound and smell of rain, he felt cheated.

He padded around his now noticeably dingy apartment for a couple of hours, doing chores and fixing his dad and him some breakfast. They shared idle conversation over a cup of coffee and scrambled eggs. Then Eli switched gears.

"Dad, have you thought any more about trying another rehab?" Just looking at his dad made Eli's heart ache. He seemed much older than his fifty-five years. A life wasted. Alcohol was his drug of choice so he could stop feeling.

"I've tried. Why waste the money? I am what I am." His bloodshot eyes held deep sadness.

"No, Dad, this isn't who you are. I remember—"

"That man is gone. He died a long time ago." His dad rose and headed into the living room, switching on the tube and effectively ending any further conversation.

The boys showed up one by one. By eleven o'clock, seven middle schoolers, his dad, and he were sharing one plaid couch, a matching easy chair, and most of the floor space, all attempting to focus on a football game playing on a TV the size of an old record album.

The youth center popped into his head for about the tenth time. It had to be better than this, but he knew if he took them once, they'd want to go back all the time. Was he willing to listen to the God-thing for their sakes? *Ah. . .why not? It would beat this scenario.*

Eli instructed the boys to go tell their moms they'd be with him the rest of the day. He'd have them home by nine and would escort them to their doors.

Their excitement was worth his personal discomfort. *Hope I don't live to regret this day.*

Arriving at the center, his brood nearly charged the door. Once inside, they headed in fifty directions. They were like kids turned loose in a candy store.

He searched the room for Delanie, a little embarrassed to be there after his uncharacteristic emotional tirade yesterday. He spotted her over by the tables and chairs near the kitchen, talking to a rookie he'd seen at the station a couple of times.

Her gaze connected with his, and she sent a welcoming smile his way. His heart did a little dance, and a moment later she headed toward him.

"Hey, you, I'm so glad you came. Did you bring the guys?"

"Seven of them."

About that time Oscar and Miguel approached. "Hi, Delanie," they said in unison. Both wore face-splitting grins, and admiration was written all over their boyish faces.

Delanie welcomed them. "If you'll excuse us," she said to Eli, "I have two important guests I'd like to show around and introduce to a few people." She made their day. Lately, just seeing her made his. He shook his head, trying to rid himself of the unwelcome thought.

Eli saw her dad playing foosball, Sarge standing over near the video games, and her brother Frank Jr. playing a board game at the far end of the room. Several other cops were scattered around the room, and they all wore bright green T-shirts that said "Cops-N-Kidz" in huge letters on their backs. Delanie carried one and was headed toward him.

"Where are Oscar and Miguel?"

"I lost them in the media room. The Star Wars trilogy is playing today."

"We won't see them again for hours." He reached for the lime green shirt. "Where can I help?" Eli glanced around, but all of the areas appeared well monitored.

Delanie scrunched her nose. "How good of a sport are you?"

"Depends. Why?"

"We're short in the kitchen today. Two people called in sick."

Eli groaned. "The kitchen? You mean no video games, no Star Wars?"

"That's what I mean. You in or not?"

"I suppose." He let out a long sigh as if the assignment were more than he could bear. Then he winked. "I take it I'm supposed to put this on?" He held up the bright shirt.

"Yeah, makes it easy for the kids to spot a leader if they need one."

"Green's *not* my color," he joked, heading for the restroom to change. "I'll meet you in the kitchen in five."

The place was bright and cheery, and even with all of the commotion and noise, Eli sensed a peace there. And Delanie... Things were changing between them. He'd lost his hostile edge. It felt as if they were on the cusp of friendship. He hadn't had a friend in a very long time.

A couple of minutes later, he joined Delanie in the kitchen. She introduced him to her mother and her sister-in-law, Sunnie. After everyone was served hot dogs, hamburgers, french fries, and baked beans, Chief Cooper said it was his turn to share the message.

Someone dragged out a little mock stage that put him a couple of feet higher, along with a metal music stand. "I hate standing on this thing." He hooked a little mic on the neck of his T-shirt and clipped the box to the back of his jeans. "But it makes it easier for everybody to see me, and it makes me feel taller." He picked up the metal stand and moved it all the way to the edge. "I don't need this thing. I'm not going to use any notes," he informed the guy who'd carried it out.

This was the part Eli dreaded, where they'd try to cram Jesus down everyone's throat. He searched for an escape route, but there was none to be had. *I wonder how they'll try to guilt us all into this.*

nine

"I want to speak on the sovereignty of God," Chief Cooper began. "Being a cop, I have to tell you I often wonder, why do bad things happen to good people? And I also question, why do good things happen to bad people? Doesn't make much sense to me—does it to you?"

None at all, Eli agreed.

"I see the single mother working two jobs just so her kids can eat and live in a rat-infested apartment complex. Meanwhile, the drug lord resides across town in a mansion with servants and enough money to buy anything he could ever want. Where's God? Where's fair?"

Eli noted that all of his brood sat together in a clump at one table. They were in front of him, so he couldn't see their faces, but they, like everyone in the room, were still and attentive. That said a lot for Chief Cooper's speaking skills.

"I don't know about you, but that used to bug me—a lot—until I settled the whole thing with God through studying His Word. I'll tell you what I discovered. . . ."

Eli realized Delanie must have mentioned the "Where was God?" questions Eli had shouted at her yesterday; otherwise, why would her dad broach the subject? *Should have known not to trust her.* He glanced over at her, but her attention was solely on her dad, admiration highlighting her expression.

Eli refocused on Chief Cooper.

"God did create a perfect world for us to live in. The whole account is in the early part of the book of Genesis—if you care to, read it yourself later. There was no sickness, no death, no sorrow, no shame. Then Adam and Eve disobeyed God, choosing to consume the fruit He'd told them to leave alone. How many times do we do the exact opposite of what a parent or teacher asks? I know I had that tendency, especially when I was younger.

"But by sinning, disobeying, doing wrong, Adam and Eve ushered evil into the perfect world God provided. Along with their action came sickness, death, and every form of wickedness. So now because of man's choices, not because of God's lack of provision, we live in a fallen and imperfect world."

Chief Cooper moved around as he spoke, looking into each face. "With cancer, killing—the list goes on and on. But the Bible says it's temporary. Do you know why?"

Some nodded yes, some no. Eli knew why. Jesus. He'd gone to church as a kid, even asked Jesus into his heart. But if a *loving* God didn't care about a twelve-year-old boy, Eli didn't need Him. Anger surged through him.

"If God gave His very own, one and only Son to die in your place, there's nothing He wouldn't do for you. Absolutely nothing."

Except save my brother's life. Make my mother stay when I needed her so much. Eli swallowed, trying to dislodge the lump in his throat.

"Now I'm certain some of you are doubting my words. I see it on your faces. You're thinking, *If what the chief is saying is true, why did my grandpa die or my parents divorce or my mom get beat up?* I guarantee you, none of that is God's will, but every man, woman, and child on the planet has a free will. Each person chooses for himself what his actions and reactions will be. Like the law of gravity—if you drop something from a second-story window, it will splat to the ground. God could override that law of nature but doesn't. You touch a hot stove—you will get burned."

You take too many drugs—you die.

"Bad things happen. Not because God wills them, but because we or other people choose them."

Ronny chose to take more drugs than was medically possible for him to survive. Maybe it wasn't God's fault. The thought was new to him. He felt the words chiseling away inside his chest, chipping down the walls he'd placed around his heart. Chief Cooper asked everyone to bow his or her head; then he said a prayer, but Eli didn't hear. He was too busy with his own. *God, if You're real, and if what Chief Cooper says is true, show me. Please show me.*

Eli wanted to believe, wanted what he saw in Delanie. Was it possible?

He and his posse headed outside after the message to shoot some hoops. The rain had stopped, though it was still cloudy and windy. Several other guys joined them. Eli avoided Delanie the rest of the day, lest she want to play twenty questions about her dad's talk.

At eight he rounded up his crew, and they said good-bye. Amid their protests they loaded into the van and headed toward home. Once the van was rolling, Oscar asked, "Hey, Eli, what you thinkin' 'bout that Jesus dude?"

He'd been thinking a lot about Him all afternoon but wasn't sure what to say to the boy. Eli's head was mixed up; he didn't want to confuse the kid, as well.

"He sounds like a good guy."

"You ever heard of Him before?" one of the boys in the very back hollered.

" 'Course," Miguel answered. "My grandma has pictures of Him in her house. We go to Mass."

"You heard of Him, Eli?" Oscar asked.

"Yeah, I went to Sunday school as a kid."

Eli listened but didn't say much. What *was* he thinking about that Jesus dude? He had no idea, but for the first time in almost twenty years, he was thinking about Him. He wished he could go home and ask his dad, but he rarely saw him. He spent about twelve hours a day at the bar and the rest sleeping it off. Sometimes, like now, Eli ached for someone to talk to. They used to go to church as a family. Why did they quit, and what did his dad believe about God?

❧

Delanie and Eli fell into a comfortable routine. During the week they began their stakeout of various lawyers, and on weekends they spent their time at the youth center. Delanie was dying to know what Eli thought about the various messages and testimonies he'd heard, but she refused to allow herself to pry. If and when he chose to share with her, she'd love to listen, but it really was between him and God.

Delanie pulled up in front of Walden's. She'd been surprised when Courtney called and wanted to get together. Courtney had all but disappeared the past three months or so.

"Hey, Court." Delanie made a beeline for the table and gave her old friend a big hug. "I've missed you, girl. How have you been?"

Courtney literally glowed. "Wonderful." She held out her left hand and flashed a large diamond under Delanie's nose. "I'm engaged."

Delanie so wanted to be happy for her, but how could she be? Her heart weighed heavy in her chest. "Wow, so you are." *Lord, help me know what to say.* "This is quick. Are you sure?"

"Three months is long enough to know." Courtney's tone was defensive. "Truly, it was love at first sight."

Delanie thought of her own timeline with Eli. Yes, three months was enough time to know. Only she and Eli wouldn't have a fairy-tale ending. There'd be no happily ever after. She doubted Courtney would have that experience either, even if she married the guy. They could never truly be one in the spiritual aspect. Blessing follows obedience, just as havoc often marks disobedience. She wished she could make Courtney see that principle.

"So when's the big day?" Delanie hoped Courtney would wait at least a year. She'd read it takes a full twelve months to begin to see each facet of a personality.

"We're talking spring, maybe April."

Delanie bit her lip. "You won't have known him long, less than a year."

"True. About eight months, though, and when you're in love, what does it matter?"

Delanie considered giving her the whole list of reasons to wait but chose not to waste her breath.

"Anyway." Courtney laid her hand on Delanie's arm. "Will you be my maid of honor?"

Delanie smiled, touched that Courtney felt so close to her, and then panic hit her. Would it be wrong to stand up for her friend when she didn't agree with her decision? Or did a true friend shut up and mind her own business?

"You are my oldest and dearest friend." Courtney must have assumed Delanie's smile meant acceptance. "We've known each other since what?"

"Third grade."

"And third grade was about twenty years ago. Over two-thirds of our lives."

Delanie nodded. Even way back when, Courtney never had a hair out of place and always had boys on her mind.

"I never thought I'd be the first one of our group to marry!" Courtney was positively giddy. She stared at her ring. "Can you believe it, D? I'm getting married, and you're going to be my maid of honor!"

No, frankly, she couldn't believe it. This was all happening way too fast, for Courtney and for her. She didn't even know if she wanted the maid of honor position.

"Now tell me about you and the detective fellow. Are you going to race me to the altar?"

Had Courtney not heard a thing she'd said a few months ago? "I told you, I won't date an unbeliever." Delanie's words sounded harsher than she'd intended.

"Tad goes to church with me every Sunday." Courtney refolded her napkin so the crease was exactly in the center.

"You know that doesn't make him a Christian. You're still unequally yoked." Delanie wished she were better at speaking the truth in love; for some reason she always ended up sounding self-righteous.

"He's not now, but he will be. You just watch and see." Irritation wove itself through Courtney's words.

"I hope so—for your sake, I really do."

Jodi and Kristen joined them at the table, and Courtney went through the whole story all over again. Neither of them seemed thrilled either but tried to simulate excitement. Their mouths nearly fell open when Courtney announced Delanie would be her maid of honor. Then she asked them to be her two bridesmaids. They, too, agreed, though Delanie sensed the same uncertainty in them that she wrestled with.

Jodi and Kristen returned to the table with their coffees in tow when Courtney rose. "Hey," she said, glancing at her watch. "I've got to run. I'm having dinner with Tad." She slipped her purse strap over her shoulder. "Thanks for being in my wedding. We'll get together later and pick dresses and all that fun stuff." She hugged each of them and was gone.

Jodi and Kristen were both wide-eyed, mirroring what Delanie felt.

"What just happened here?" Kristen frowned.

Jodi shook her head. "Did Courtney, or did Courtney not, invite all of us to join her for dinner?"

Delanie laughed. "Apparently Dr. Dreamboat must take precedence."

"They're getting married." Jodi's tone sounded as if someone had died.

"I know, and instead of rejoicing with her, we're all saddened by her big announcement." Delanie sipped her mocha.

"What should we do?" Kristen asked.

"I wish I knew." Delanie let out a long sigh. "Last time we got together, I explained why it wasn't a good idea and told her why I can't let my attraction to Eli get out of hand."

"Speaking of. . ." Kristen raised her brow. "He is pretty cute, in a rugged-looking actor sort of way."

"You've seen him?" Jodi asked. Then her accusing glare settled on Delanie.

"Kristen got some information for our case, so we grabbed a quick latte."

"So what does he look like?" Jodi quizzed Kristen.

"Not Delanie's type—that's for sure."

"What is my type?"

"Clean-cut, short hair, well dressed. Everything Eli isn't." Kristen recited the list Delanie once thought described her kind of man.

"You make him sound like a bum off the street." Her hackles rose.

Jodi patted Delanie's hand. "A little defensive, aren't we?"

"No, no." Kristen held up her hand like a crossing guard. "I didn't mean it to sound negative. The guy is very good-looking. His hair isn't long like the hippie look, and he's not toting a ponytail or anything, but it's not that close-cropped look you usually go for—he's sort of shaggy around the edges."

"Like Tom at church?" Jodi asked.

"Exactly. And Eli isn't clean-shaven either." Kristen glanced at Delanie. "Not that that's a bad thing."

"Another Delanie requirement, though," Jodi reminded her. "Does he have a beard? Because you hate beards."

"No beard," Kristen assured Jodi. "Just scruffy. You know that shaved-two-days-ago look?"

"I would think kissing a guy like that could be rough on the face." Jodi rubbed her fingers across her chin and waggled her eyebrows at Delanie.

"You guys make me sound like a stern taskmaster. No wonder I'm still single at twenty-eight," Delanie joked. Then she grew serious. "I've fallen in love with him."

"For real?" Kristen asked.

"Wow." Jodi's brown eyes reflected a million questions.

"Don't worry. I'm not following in Courtney's footsteps, but it happened nonetheless. One thing I've learned—it's easy to have all the answers until you're faced with the questions."

"What about him? What's he feeling?" Jodi asked.

Delanie smiled, and her heart responded, as it always did, with a warm feeling when she let her thoughts wander to Eli. "He's gone from open hostility toward me to a cozy friendship. Sometimes when he looks at me, I see all the unnamed emotions I'm wrestling with, but he guards them closely, just as I do."

"This must be really hard. I'm so sad for you."

Jodi's compassionate response brought unexpected tears. "Me, too." Delanie dabbed at her eyes with her napkin. "I've waited my whole life for the moment I'd fall in love." She could no longer stop the tears. "And my heart betrayed me, falling for a guy I can never have."

Jodi held one of Delanie's hands and gave a little squeeze. "It's breaking my heart to see you go through this." Her eyes were teary, as well.

"Do you think this is some kind of test? Kind of like Job. Maybe God's saying, 'I know Delanie will stand in obedience no matter what's thrown her way.'" Kristen sniffed.

Delanie dried her cheeks and smiled at her dearest friends in all the world. "I don't know. Maybe I'm just in the wrong place at the wrong time. But I'll tell you what I do know—I know why my mom says Christians must be very careful about opening their hearts to non-Christians of the opposite sex. She calls it missionary dating and says it dangerous. For the first time I really understand why. The better I get to know Eli and the more I pray for him, the deeper my feelings run."

"Mother knows best," Kristen quipped.

"The sad thing is, for you, this whole trip down lovers' lane has been completely innocent." Jodi released her hand.

"Yeah. It's not like you chose to date a guy who you knew didn't know God. Work has forced you two into this relationship."

"True. But it's also opened my eyes to so much. It's easy to be self-righteous when you've never faced the temptation. If I've said it once, I've said it a million times: *I would never fall in love with someone who didn't love God as much as I do.* Not only am I in love with Eli, but he doesn't love God at all. As a matter of fact, he's antagonistic toward Him."

"That's got to be hard, especially since you have to be around him so much." Kristen toyed with her empty cup.

"I can't imagine how difficult it is for women married to guys like him." Delanie rubbed the back of her neck.

"Nor can I envision how hard Courtney's life could end up being. Why doesn't she see it?" Kristen's words were laced with discouragement.

Delanie thought about Courtney's situation. "I'm not sure any of us can see it when it's our own sin."

"You're probably right," Kristen agreed. "But if it's ever me, slap me upside the head, tie me in a closet, whatever it takes."

"Courtney's mistake was saying yes to that first invitation." Jodi looked from one to the other. "Temptation comes in just the right package whether it's a man or whatever would float our boat."

"My mom always says anything that takes our eyes off God and steals our passion can turn into sin—no matter how good or innocent the thing is. If it controls us in any way, we'll end up in trouble." Delanie was only now beginning to appreciate her mother's wisdom.

"So what do we do about Courtney?" Kristen brought the conversation full circle.

"I'm not sure there's much we can do, except pray." Delanie popped the lid off her empty cup and stuffed her napkin inside.

"Why is it that prayer sometimes feels like a passive approach, when truly it's the most aggressive approach?" Jodi tended to challenge their thinking at times. "Only God can change Courtney. We can talk until we lose our voices."

"That's the truth. I've tried to get her to think and share with her my own struggles regarding Eli, but I believe she's determined to have her own way. She's convinced herself she can have the good doctor and God, too."

"And she can." Jodi's statement surprised Delanie. "But she'll never experience the fullness God intended. I think it'll be difficult to give her whole life to God when part of it will always be tugged in another direction."

"And it'll be hard to give her whole self to her husband when he's missing the spiritual component," Kristen added.

"I feel like I need to stop the impending disaster, but as we said, only God can." Delanie shrugged her shoulders. "Let's commit to pray daily for Courtney, for Tad's salvation, and for wisdom to know if God would have us intervene in any way."

"And we'll pray for you, too," Jodi promised.

"Yeah, you're not out of the woods yet. Now let's get dinner. I'm starved." Kristen grinned.

Delanie felt better having finally unloaded her struggles on her friends. She'd thought if she refrained from voicing the feelings blooming within, they'd dissipate. Unfortunately, that wasn't the case. They were like weeds, growing bigger and stronger each day.

≈

When Eli arrived at the youth center that evening, Delanie wasn't there. Her brother said she'd taken the night off, and disappointment hit him square on. The two reasons he came here were time with the guys and more time with Delanie—a fact he hadn't acknowledged until now.

Not in the mood to talk, he grabbed a basketball and headed out back to the court. Nobody was there—which suited him just fine. The chill in the air was his ally, keeping others inside.

He shot the ball, missed it, chased it down—all the while his mind on Delanie. What should he do with these feelings clamoring around inside him? He'd never even expected to like her, let alone fall in love with her. In fact, he'd never planned to fall for anyone, not ever again. He knew women couldn't be trusted in the long haul, but somehow he couldn't quite believe that about Delanie. She was so different from anyone he'd ever known, so full of life and joy.

Something was different about most of the Christian people he'd gotten to know here at the center. The place had a calmness and a peace he sensed whenever he was there, as did the people. No one was perfect, as most were quick to admit, but all seemed centered, selfless, and crazy about God. Their outlook on life seemed foreign to him yet appealing, as well.

He dribbled the ball, pondering his unanswered questions. Were his decisions about women and God made too prematurely, before he had the answers? He shot and missed again, his focus gone. *God, are You real? Is what I'm feeling for Delanie real? And are both of you worthy of my trust, or will it be another hard lesson in the letdowns of life?*

ten

"From your reports and surveillance observations, we all agree the attorney has to be George Benavides." Sarge looked from Eli to Delanie and back again.

Eli nodded. His cop's instinct was certain.

"We haven't been able to get information from any of his clients, so it's time to try a different tack and take a more aggressive stance. We're sending Delanie in undercover."

Eli's heart stopped beating for a split second. Fear clenched his gut. "You mean both of us, right?"

Sarge shook his head. "I mean Delanie—alone. We're hoping he'll feel safer and less threatened by a single, desperate, pregnant female. Word has to have gotten back to him that we're nosing around."

"I don't think that's such a good idea." Eli didn't care for the plan and certainly didn't want Delanie put in any danger.

Delanie sat up straighter. "You still doubt my abilities as a cop?" Her question held disbelief. "Come on, Eli. When are you going to believe I can handle myself out there?" She rose from the vinyl chair and walked to the window.

"She'll be wired. I'll keep you as close as possible, only seconds away. We're checking into the office one door down the hall. It appears to be vacant. We'll have several officers in the building, ready to respond, should the need arise."

Eli nodded. He knew he was overreacting, but Delanie mattered to him—too much. Definitely much more than a partner should.

The phone rang. Sarge answered, then excused himself momentarily, leaving them alone.

Delanie glared at him from her spot by the window, arms crossed over her chest. "I can't believe after working together almost four months we're back to square one."

He fought the urge to take her into his arms and tell her he couldn't bear to lose another person, especially her. Instead, he joined her by the window.

"I have no doubt you're a good cop, far better than most I've seen."

Her expression softened when he acknowledged her abilities as a police officer. "What is your deal, then?"

What could he say? She wouldn't let up until he gave her some sort of answer. He cleared his throat. "I care about you."

Her face became guarded.

Maybe he'd misread her, because he thought she at least considered him a friend. "I don't make friends easily or lightly. Since you're one of the very few I have. . ." *The only one I have.*

Her face relaxed, and she smiled, sending his heart sailing.

"I only want you safe."

"Thank you." Her voice sounded croaky. "For counting me as a friend. I feel the same about you. And thanks for acknowledging that I'm a good cop. That means more than you know and rarely happens around here."

"Don't let it go to your head." He smiled, hoping to lighten things up. The mood was getting far too sappy for his comfort.

Sarge reentered the office, stopping just inside the doorway. His head tipped a tad to the side, and his gaze bounced from one to the other. "Things okay in here?"

"Fine," they both answered, sounding like kids caught with their hands in the cookie jar.

Sarge raised his brows, nodded, and took his chair behind the desk. "This is the way we'll play this out." He began detailing the plan. Delanie and Eli returned to the chairs, both listening to their instructions. Eli still hated sending her in alone.

"Delanie, if you want to head downstairs, they'll get you wired and ready to roll. I'll go over the building plans with Eli."

"Sure." She headed out the door.

"Something going on between you two?"

Eli shook his head. *Only in my heart.*

"The scene I walked in on looked pretty intimate."

"How? We were standing together by the window—nothing more."

"Maybe it was the rapturous expression on each of your faces, the air crackling with emotion, that misled me."

Eli's heart took flight. Based on Sarge's observations, maybe Delanie's feelings ran deeper than she was willing to admit. . . .

"So why do you object to her going in alone?" Sarge pressed.

Eli rubbed the back of his neck, trying to work out a knot. "I don't want to take any unnecessary risks—with her or with me."

"That's your story?"

"Yep."

"You know department policy. You two can't work together and be involved. I'd have to transfer one of you to another unit."

Eli knew. He also knew he'd failed to convince Sarge, but other than unspoken attraction, nothing was going on between them.

Sarge went over the blueprints with Eli, showing him where the two other cops would be. They'd all be connected to Delanie's wire, just as Eli would. An officer had confirmed that the space across the hall was vacant, so they'd secured permission to use it. Eli needed to dress the part of a businessman in case he ran into anyone in the hall. "Don't want to raise suspicions."

"Will you let Delanie know I ran home to change?"

Sarge nodded.

"Tell her I'll meet her back here at noon."

❧

Joe had to leave for a lunch appointment, so Delanie waited in his empty office for Eli. All sorts of emotions swirled through her—excitement and anticipation over their assignment this afternoon, and tenderness over Eli's declarations. For a moment she'd feared he was going to proclaim his love or something awful like that. If he did, she'd have to reject him, and hurting Eli would just kill her. Looking back, she knew that was a crazy notion. She did, however, feel blessed that he counted her among his friends.

"Delanie? You awake?" Eli startled her.

"Sorry. Daydreaming." When she turned away from the window to walk out the door, she stopped midstride, and her heart shifted into overdrive. Eli had gotten his hair cut, had shaved, and wore a gray business suit. "Wow. You clean up nice."

He struck a model-type pose. "You like?"

She nodded. His new look only increased the attraction.

"Sarge said I needed to dress the part."

"And dress the part you did. I hardly recognized you."

Eli held the door open for her, made his way around the car, and climbed in. He turned the key; the engine roared to life.

Eli pulled into traffic while Delanie updated him. "I tried

to make an appointment to see the lawyer, but his receptionist informed me he doesn't do adoptions, which I find interesting since a large percentage of the clientele we watched coming and going while staking out his office were indeed pregnant. Anyway, then it hit me: He isn't on the adoption list, but the 'George list.' I think Brandi tried to help without helping, if you know what I mean."

Eli pondered that idea. "It never occurred to me that George was a clue. Good work, Detective." His smile told her how proud he was of her. "What is plan B?"

"Sarge said grab lunch, look over the blueprints he gave you, and you can fill me in on that end of things. At three, when the attorney's office reopens after lunch and court, he wants me to be there—upset, crying, I hope, and insisting that my friend told me to come. Do you think I should use Brandi's name? Or just pick a really common name and hope it rings true with him?"

Delanie looked up from her notes and discovered he'd brought her to Bertha's for lunch. "You're scoring all sorts of points with me today," she joked as he opened her car door and helped her out. "You compliment my ability as a cop, bring me to my favorite restaurant, and promote me to your friend list." She dared not also mention how attractive she found him in his new getup.

While they waited for a table, they talked about the youth center and how much his group of junior highers loved being there. "What about you? You've never told me what you think of the place."

He shrugged. "It's okay." The subject seemed to make him uncomfortable.

Delanie nodded.

"I mean, it's a great place for the guys, and I appreciate

everyone welcoming them and making us all feel right at home. Don't get me wrong—I'm grateful."

"Do you miss having more time—just you and them?"

"I do."

The host called them and led them down a few steps to the back of the room and a little booth for two.

Eli looked up. "I hadn't noticed this before." The ceiling on this part of the restaurant wasn't wood like the rest, but Plexiglas.

"It's kind of weird being inside yet seeing the sky overhead, isn't it? I think my dad said they added this part later. See the half wall with the large pots on it? That used to be the outside wall. My favorite time to come, though, is in the summer when they open their outdoor patio and you can eat outside in the shade of a big tree."

"You're an outdoor girl at heart, aren't you?"

Delanie nodded. "One reason I chose this job."

"Do you hunt?"

"I have with my dad." She scrunched her face. "I don't enjoy the blood-and-guts part of it. Fishing's the same way. I don't mind the catching part but hate the cleaning part. How about you?"

"I do love any outdoor sport, and I like spectator sports, as well. I'm a huge Angels fan."

"So I noticed by your caps and attire." She winked at him.

"Guess I'm not the classiest guy around, huh?"

"I think you're pretty classy, at least in the ways that matter. Any single guy who dedicates his life to a group of neighborhood kids is the classiest."

The smile he shined on her jump-started her heart.

The waiter arrived with hot plates of food, interrupting the moment.

Delanie took a bite of her enchiladas. "Do you think I should mention Brandi's name when I get to the lawyer's office," she asked again, "or will that draw suspicion?"

"I'm not sure, but let's err on the side of safe rather than sorry. I'm afraid mentioning Brandi's name might increase wariness. What's a fairly common girl's name?"

"Amanda, Melissa. I don't know. Maybe I'll try not to mention a name but just refer to 'my friend.'"

They ate lunch and chitchatted. Delanie loved their easy conversations. If not for her attraction, she'd love to work with Eli forever; but as things stood, she'd decided that when the case closed, she'd request a new assignment. Sarge would understand.

Eli paid the bill. Their short drive to the bank building was quiet. She was planning what to say, and Eli was engrossed in thought, as well.

Eli had never experienced so much apprehension about an undercover assignment before. He hated Sarge's plan and wished he had tried harder to dissuade him. His feelings for Delanie were messing with his mind and impairing his judgment as a cop. This was the first case ever where he wasn't willing to get the guy whatever the cost. He could barely stand the thought of her going in alone.

The irony of the situation was that when they started this case, he worried about Delanie's ability to handle things, but now he was the one struggling to keep a cool head and stay unemotional about her safety on the case. If there was a God, He must have a sense of humor.

"I'm going to park in this garage, which is a couple of blocks away. Right outside the garage is a bus stop where you can wait while we get set up."

Eli drove all the way to the roof of the garage. Only three cars were up there—all empty—and not a soul to be seen. He pulled into a spot, gave Delanie last-minute instructions, and got out to walk her to the elevator.

He struggled to let her go through with the plan. He couldn't bear the thought of something happening to her, and he knew these people weren't afraid of murder.

Delanie reached for the elevator button, and he grabbed her hand. "Wait."

Her brows drew together as she studied him. "What?"

I'm in love with her, totally and completely. Fully acknowledging all of the feelings floating around in his heart caused Eli to throw caution to the wind. He pulled her into his arms and watched several emotions play across her features. The first was surprise, but as his lips found hers, he saw the same longing he felt.

He pulled her close, which wasn't close enough at all with her fake tummy between them. As the kiss deepened, he wondered how it had taken him so long to recognize the love between them. She felt it, too; he was sure of it.

When the kiss ended, he held her tight for several seconds and whispered her name.

She pushed out of his arms. Her expression reminded him of a deer in headlights—dazed and confused. "What are we doing?"

"I have feelings for you, and I wanted—"

"Don't!" She backed up a couple of steps, just out of his reach. "Don't have feelings for me." She pushed the elevator button and turned accusing eyes on him. "I asked you not to *ever* kiss me again." Her voice grew demanding. "Now I'm telling you—never again! You got it?" She pointed her index finger at him.

The elevator doors opened, and she stepped inside. He blocked the doors from sliding shut. "I read you loud and clear." The truth was, he'd completely misread her. "Turn on your body pack so we can make sure our gear is working." They both reached behind them and slid the little buttons over. "Testing."

Delanie nodded that his voice had come over the wire. "Testing," she said in a shaky voice.

"We're good." Eli walked away, and the elevator whisked Delanie off.

He wondered how he'd so utterly misinterpreted her. He leaned against the car to catch his breath and regroup. Though his feelings ran deep, hers obviously didn't. He shook his head, struggling to reconcile her words with the tender looks she sometimes gave him and the kiss they'd shared moments before with this end result. He climbed in the car, slamming the door. Now he remembered why he'd avoided women— none of them made a bit of sense.

❧

Delanie couldn't chase away the memory of the hurt expression she'd brought to Eli's face. It broke her heart to treat him so callously, but she didn't know what else to do.

Exiting the elevator, she took a seat on the bench at the bus stop. She couldn't very well tell him she had feelings for him, too, but because of her relationship with God, she'd have to ignore those emotions. He already hated God enough without her adding more ammunition. Then he'd not only blame God for his brother's death and his mother's leaving, but blame God for their failed relationship, too.

She also couldn't risk telling him the truth in case he decided to become a Christian just so they could start dating. Nope, that was never a good idea. A true conversion had to happen between a man and God, not with the motive of a woman behind it.

The one plus from this mess—Delanie would have no trouble crying in the lawyer's office. She was on the verge now.

A bus pulled up, and the door opened. Shaking her head, she waved it on.

"Then get off my bench, lady," the driver yelled. He shut his door and drove off, leaving Delanie to choke on the bus's exhaust. She rose and started walking toward the bank building.

Eli pulled out of the garage and passed her. "Don't enter the building until you're told." His voice had a hard edge to it. "Copy?"

"Copy." She wanted to find a quiet corner somewhere and bawl her eyes out, but three other guys heard everything she did, so she'd have to be tough and save the tears for later. *Buck up, little buckaroo.*

She walked to Dreamer's and ordered an iced blended mocha. The other two cops teased her and complained about sitting in a hot stairwell while she lived the good life. Eli, however, said nary a word.

Delanie grabbed a table outside and watched the river rush by, wishing she could follow it somewhere far away from heartbreak. Even worse than her own sorrow was knowing she'd hurt Eli. He'd opened his heart for the first time in a long time and offered not only his friendship, but more, and because of circumstances beyond her control, she cruelly shoved the deal back in his face. She knew instinctively they'd no longer share the lighthearted relationship she'd come to love. Eli would shut her out, and their tenuous buds of friendship would not survive today.

Lord, please heal his hurts and touch him with Your love. Send someone who'll adore him and then draw them both to You.

Delanie wiped a silent tear from her cheek.

"Cooper, we're in place. Keep us apprised of your approach." Eli was all business.

Digging through her purse, Delanie said, "I'm leaving the river walk. ETA at the front door in two minutes." Once she finished talking, she closed her oversize handbag. Rummaging through it provided a good distraction for conversing without anyone's being able to tell.

She entered the building and pressed the elevator button. She was the only one in it, so she freely said, "Approaching the third floor."

"Copy," echoed in her ear three times.

"This will be my last update, so unless I say different, assume all is going according to plan." Delanie grabbed a stick of gum from her purse. "Excuse the chomping, but I'm role-playing."

She stuffed the gum in her mouth, exited the elevator, and found suite 314.

Delanie's heart pounded. She stopped by the restroom to inspect her appearance. Yep, she looked the part of a pregnant teen. She said a quick prayer and sauntered through the office door and up to the receptionist, requesting to speak to George Benavides.

"Do you have an appointment?"

Delanie chomped, shaking her head back and forth.

"I'm sorry. Without an appointment he can't see you."

Delanie pictured Eli's face when she pushed him away and rejected his offering of something more. This time she could let the tears fall, and fall they did.

"I tried to make an appointment, but you wouldn't let me." She spoke loudly to draw the attention and, she hoped, sympathy of the onlookers.

"Miss, please calm down." The receptionist spoke in a quiet, calm tone. "Mr. Benavides doesn't handle adoptions. Isn't that why you're here? I explained that to you on the phone when you called earlier."

Delanie cried harder, for Brandi, for Julie, for Eli. "He does. I know he does. A girl I met on the bus told me he'd help me find a wonderful home for my baby. Another girl I met in the mall told me the same thing." Delanie sobbed. "Why are you lying to me?"

Two security guards entered the office. The receptionist must have pushed some sort of button to summon them. Delanie hadn't counted on that.

"Please show this young lady out and see that she doesn't return."

The men each took an arm and escorted her all the way to the front door of the building. "You'd best heed our warning, miss. Don't come back, or we'll handle you more severely next time."

Delanie nodded.

"Head to the garage," Eli's voice boomed through her earpiece. "I'm in section 4B. I'll meet you at the car."

All of the emotion of the day wore on her. She wanted to go home, soak in a hot tub, and shed a few tears. Oh, how she wished she could unbreak a couple of hearts.

eleven

Delanie was already waiting when he got to the car. She looked a mess, her face red and blotchy, her eyes swollen. She didn't say a word, which was fine by him. He'd foolishly thought she cared. He'd obviously failed to learn his lesson well enough, but this would be the last time he'd ever open himself to anyone.

He pushed the number 3 on his cell phone and unlocked her door.

"Eli, how'd things come down?" Sarge asked.

Eli recounted the afternoon.

"You two head home. We'll put our heads together and devise a new plan in the morning."

"Will do." Eli shut his phone and slipped it into the pocket inside his suit jacket. When he pulled to a stop in front of Delanie's place, he relayed what Sarge had said.

She nodded. "I think I'll drive myself in to work tomorrow morning. I've got some errands and stuff. . ."

Relieved, he agreed. "Yeah, that's probably better."

She opened her door.

"Delanie?"

She paused.

He hated to ask but had to know.

"Are you going to the center tonight?"

"No. I think I'm going to take a break for a while."

Good. "When you decide to go, if you'll give me the heads-up, I'll stay out of your hair."

She inclined her head in acknowledgment. "Bye, Eli." Her words sounded so final, and his heart hurt with the loss. *What went wrong?* He didn't have a clue.

He was relieved she planned to take a break from Cops-N-Kidz. The guys loved going there, and frankly, so did he. Some unknown something inside him craved more of what he found there—the joy, the peace, even the messages that uplifted instead of condemned. His brood felt the same way, and they often ended up there four or five times a week. Tonight was no different. The vote was unanimous, and they loaded up the van and headed over, stopping at the Burger House on the way.

Sarge delivered tonight's message, and his words were powerful. He spoke about God's amazing, immeasurable, unconditional love for each person in the room. "No matter what you look like, how unlovable you feel, God adores each one of you. The Bible calls us—all people everywhere—the apple of God's eye!"

Eli felt a tug on his heartstrings but chalked it up to a long day and Delanie's rejection.

At the end Sarge invited people forward to receive Christ. Oscar and Jose both responded to the invitation. Eli envied their childlike faith, wishing it were that easy as an adult to simply believe.

ᐧᐧ

The following morning Eli made his way to Sarge's office, wishing he didn't have to face Delanie after his foolish proclamation yesterday. Talk about a man with regrets.

Yet there she was in the midst of a serious conversation with Sarge. Were they talking about him?

When Delanie saw him, she smiled, one of those ear-to-ear jobs that lit her whole face. "Sarge said Oscar and Jose accepted Christ last night! That's so wonderful!" She bubbled over with excitement.

So that was what they'd been talking about. Probably wondering when he'd take the plunge. He decided a change of topic was in order. "Anybody come up with a plan yet?"

"We need to get an undercover worker into the office." Sarge focused on him. "Any ideas?"

"It would have to be entry level." Eli took the seat next to Delanie. "Cleaning service? Night security for the whole building?"

"What about the receptionist?" Delanie paced to the window. "The person who has direct access to all files."

Sarge nodded. "Could work."

Skeptical, Eli reminded them, "That lady was no-nonsense and pretty hard-nosed. I'm not sure she'd roll over easily."

"Let's check the angles." Sarge grabbed a pen and jotted as he spoke. "Eli, you check out the building, both security and cleaning. Who does it, what sort of access they have to files, and the like."

Pointing his pen at Delanie, he continued, "Find out everything there is to know about the receptionist. We'll meet back here tomorrow morning and make the best plan with all the info available. Agreed?"

A day without Delanie—he'd more than agree.

&

The next morning Eli and Delanie met in Sarge's office. He was there first. She blamed the line at the coffee shop for holding her up.

"So what did you discover?" Sarge gazed in Eli's direction.

"The janitorial service cleans the building every Saturday."

"That's out. We'd stall the case for another week." His eyes shifted. "Delanie?"

"The receptionist, Lisa Konica, is a single mom with two teenage boys. Both have had minor scrimmages with the law. She needs her job. I think she's the way for us to go." She glanced at Eli, looking as if she expected an argument.

"What's your plan?" Sarge asked.

Delanie shared her idea.

"You have anything better?"

Eli shook his head. "The night guard wouldn't necessarily have access to files."

"All right, then. You two head out and conquer the world. Get the warrants and paperwork in place. I'll arrange for a temp to step in this afternoon. I know the perfect police-woman for the job. Name's Mildred. She'll whip their office into shape in no time."

"We'll get it all done before noon," Eli promised.

They took care of all of the arrangements and at noon were waiting outside the bank building to tail the receptionist. Other than the frosty silence, she and Eli were still simpatico. They worked well together. And other than the empty ache in her heart and the sadness in his eyes, she could almost pretend life was status quo.

"She's leaving the building," announced an officer planted near the elevator on the third floor. Eli glanced at Delanie, and she gave him a nod, letting him know her earpiece worked and she'd heard.

Another announcement came from the cop planted on the first floor. Eli had parked near the receptionist's car, and they'd trail her off the property in case those security goons were anywhere near the site.

The plan was flowing perfectly. Lisa Konica climbed into her car and drove out. Eli followed at a respectable distance.

"Target en route. Thanks, guys," Delanie said into the radio.

"Over and out, then."

"Wonder where she'll go for lunch."

Eli didn't respond to her ponderings other than giving a shrug.

The woman drove toward Delanie's part of town, turning into Plum Tree Plaza.

"I'll bet she's going to Emerald City."

꙾

Eli glanced up at the sign. EMERALD CITY ESPRESSO & TEA CAFÉ. No surprise Delanie knew about this place. Any spot in Reno that sold designer coffee, she had a handle on.

The receptionist entered the restaurant with her purse and a book. "Let's give her space—let her order and settle in. Then we'll join her."

"Okay."

They waited a few minutes to walk in, then got in line to order at the counter. Delanie wore a cap and had her hair up. Without the belly and her trademark hair, they figured the woman wouldn't recognize her until they approached.

Eli perused the whiteboard with the menu printed on it. They had soups, salads, sandwiches, quiches, and pastries. Girl food, if you asked him. Delanie would call this place quaint; he, however, thought it was just plain weird, yuppified to the max.

The one nice touch was a fireplace with a roaring fire. Perhaps Ms. Konica would grab one of those plush couches near the fire.

Once she ordered, she settled in a cozy chair in the corner and opened her book. He and Delanie ordered drinks and sat in a chair on each side of the unsuspecting receptionist.

"Excuse me." Delanie removed her hat, her silky locks falling over her shoulders.

"You! Get out of here right now, or I'm calling the police," Ms. Konica hissed.

"At your service." Eli whipped out his badge. Delanie followed his lead.

Ms. Konica swallowed hard and laid down her book. "What is this about?"

"Your employer." Delanie leaned forward. "What can you tell us about his activities?"

"Look." She paused when the waitress brought her salad. "Thank you." Ms. Konica set the salad aside on the coffee table. "I do my job, nothing more, nothing less, and I don't get involved in the clients' personal dealings."

"Are you familiar with the term *accessory*?" Eli asked.

She glared at him. "I work for an attorney; of course I know and understand legal terms." She acted calm, but her quivering voice belied her demeanor.

"You give us what we need, and we'll keep you out of what comes down." Eli leaned toward her.

Her eyes filled with tears. "I'm a single mother, and I'm all my boys have." She sniffed. "Their dad's been MIA for years. They need me."

Delanie patted the woman's hand. "We know that, and we want to keep you out of this. There are several ways this can play out—the choice is yours. You can give us the information we seek about the baby-selling ring, or we can charge you and run you in."

Terror filled Ms. Konica's face, and Eli knew she was aware of more than she'd admitted to knowing.

Delanie continued. "You go back to work this afternoon, and we gather the needed evidence to make the bust. Choice two, you call in this afternoon with a long-term excuse—mother with cancer, death in the family far away in another state. Offer to set up a temp. We send in an undercover policewoman. In the meantime, you and your boys are taken to a safe house and kept under twenty-four-hour surveillance until this is over. It's your call."

Ms. Konica buried her face in her hands.

"I know this is tough." Eli's patience wore thin. "But you should have resigned the minute you knew your boss was involved in anything even slightly shady, let alone a class B felony."

She raised her head and glared at Eli. "That's easy for you to say. Do you have two kids to feed and no one in the world to depend on except yourself?" She spat out the words. "Mr. Benavides pays me very well."

Delanie also glared at Eli. "I'm sure what Detective Logan is trying to say is that, unfortunately, you're in a difficult position, which results from working for a man who isn't honest."

Ms. Konica nodded her head. "Can you send us to Kansas? My mother is there, and her health is failing."

Delanie glanced at Eli. He deemed her far too compassionate. "We'll see what we can do. Meanwhile, call your boss," Eli instructed.

She pulled out her cell phone, searched her phone book, and found her boss's cell number. Her hand was unsteady. She hit TALK and put the phone to her ear. "Mr. B., it's Lisa. My mom's health is failing, and I need to catch a flight to Kansas this afternoon. I'm having a temp sent in." She paused. "Thank you, sir. I'm not sure how long I'll be gone. I'll keep in touch." Her breathing was hiccuppy, indicating she'd been crying. Everything about the call rang genuine.

"Delanie, why don't you visit with Ms. Konica while I call Sarge?"

Delanie nodded and encouraged the woman to eat her lunch.

Eli stepped outside. "Sarge, Eli. Send Mildred in."

"Good job." Sarge's voice boomed over the cell phone.

"Thanks. Delanie wants to know if we can send Ms. Konica and her boys to Kansas."

"Not yet. After it goes down, we'll talk. Right now I want to keep an eye on her. Make certain she doesn't decide to alert her boss."

"Got it." Frankly, Eli didn't feel the woman deserved any special favors.

"We'll get Mildred in there and have you and Delanie posted in the office you used the other day. She'll be wired, and her code word will be *blue*. You hear 'blue'—you move."

"Yes, sir."

"I'll meet you there this afternoon, and we'll get set up. I've got warrants for video feed and bugs. The whole crew will be there at two, ready to go."

"See you at two."

Eli returned to the café. Ms. Konica was finishing her salad. Two plainclothes officers showed up to escort her to pick up the boys and get them settled.

Eli recapped his phone conversation with Sarge on his and Delanie's drive back. He dropped her off to change into a business suit, then ran home to do the same. When he picked her up not thirty minutes later, they headed back to the bank building.

The afternoon bustled with activity. Luckily George Benavides had court, leaving them open access to the office for a couple of hours.

Sarge brought Mildred over for a quick introduction. Eli wasn't sure what he expected, but a chubby, fiftysomething with attitude wasn't it.

"So you two young things got my back, right?"

"Right," Eli affirmed.

Delanie echoed his answer.

"Okay, enough niceties. I've got to get over there and on the phone with Lisa Konica so I can pick her brain and learn the ropes. I gotta do this job well so old Georgie will keep me around." Mildred smiled and was gone.

By four, everything was in place. Eli and Delanie could watch the office from the monitors across the hall, seeing and hearing everything in the waiting room. They'd placed bugs in the attorney's office, as well.

"Anyone asks," Sarge informed Delanie and Eli, "you're private investigators, recently leaving a bigger firm and starting your own."

Both nodded.

"Mildred's hours are eight to five, so yours will run seven thirty to five thirty. No need to come into the station; just be here every morning with your lunch in tow. The less attention you draw to yourselves, the better, so lay low."

"Got it." Eli saluted Sarge.

"Mildred will keep her wire on until she's safely in her car. Her safety is priority one; catching the crooks is number two."

Sarge looked both Eli and Delanie up and down. "I hardly recognize you two. No need for the executive attire if you're both private eyes; so come to work tomorrow looking less like lawyers and more like MacGyver."

Eli laughed. "I'd rather look like him any day than wear these duds." He pointed at the only suit he owned.

Sarge left, and Eli and Delanie hung out watching monitors. George Benavides returned and greeted Mildred.

"He seems pleased," Delanie said, watching their inter-action on her screen.

"Yeah, what a great decoy. Who'd ever guess she's one of us?"

Delanie glanced at Eli. "Do you think he was suspicious?"

"I think anyone in his boat would have to be—all the time. That's a rotten way to live, always looking over your shoulder." Eli's own words convicted him. That was exactly how he lived—never trusting, never opening up, keeping himself closed off from anyone over fourteen, always looking over his shoulder for the next raw deal to hit his life. His heart pounded faster at the discovery.

He and Delanie waited in silence until both George and Mildred left the office. They exited together and walked to the garage. On the way George asked her about her family, how long she'd lived in Reno, those sorts of things.

"She's perfect," Delanie said in awe.

Mildred was a natural, so calm, so real, so unassuming. She bid "Georgie" good-bye at the elevator. They could hear the heels of her pumps clicking against the cement. Once Mildred was inside her car, they heard the buzzer, the engine turn over, and the seat belt click shut.

"Sitting duck safely in her car," Mildred quipped. "Until tomorrow, over and out."

"That's our cue." Eli removed his headphones and shut down his computer. "Ready?"

He drove back to the department so Delanie could pick up her car and he, his bike.

"I'll meet you in our new office in the morning. 'Night, Eli." Delanie exited her side of the car before he had a chance to get out and open her door.

"See ya."

He decided to go straight to the youth center. Tonight was labeled family night, so all of the guys stayed home, helped with chores, played games, whatever. He was teaching them to initiate relationships and make things happen within their families. He recognized the irony in that but wanted them to have better memories than he did as a boy.

When Eli entered the center, he spotted Chief Cooper. Eli sauntered over to him, hoping to appear casual. Inside, a million questions rolled around. "I was hoping you'd be here. Can we talk?"

"You bet." The chief shook his hand. "I haven't taken the time to tell you how good it is to have you and your brood here so often."

So he'd noticed.

"Let's go in the office. We can shut the door and have some privacy."

Eli had never been in the office. It contained a desk and two upholstered chairs. The chief settled in one and motioned for Eli to do the same.

"What's on your mind, son?"

twelve

Eli sat in one of the wingback chairs facing the chief. "I had some questions regarding your message a few weeks ago—why bad things happen to good people and vice versa."

"I'll do my best to answer."

"I assume Delanie already told you my story and my struggles with God."

The chief had a blank expression. "No. The only thing she's shared with me is your expertise as a cop and how much she's enjoyed working with you."

Though he fought it, the revelation touched his heart with that warm, fuzzy Delanie feeling. "I just assumed you taught that lesson because I'd shared those same questions with your daughter the day before."

Chief Cooper smiled. "Purely a God-thing, son. I had no idea you struggled with those issues, but God knew. Maybe He's beckoning you to Himself. Did He use me to answer some of your questions?"

"God knew. Maybe He's beckoning you. . ." The words reverberated through his head and his heart. *You're proving to me that You're real, aren't You?* "You answered some of my questions, but now I have even more." Eli filled him in on the details of his background—the ugly truths of his life.

The chief's compassionate eyes matched his daughter's exactly. "I'm sorry, son. No boy of twelve should have to deal with those kinds of things. I'd stake my life on the fact that God's heart was as broken as yours. I believe His perfect plan for twelve-year-old boys would be flying kites and playing with puppies, not drugs, funerals, and missing mothers."

His words brought tears to Eli's eyes but also comfort to his heart. "If what you said is true, that bad things happen because of man's sinful choices and not because God wills them, can God forgive me for all the things I've said against Him?"

"He can, and He will. All you have to do is ask. Have you heard the story of the prodigal son?"

Eli shook his head. "I don't think so, not that I can remember, anyway."

Chief Cooper proceeded to recite the story of a boy who'd taken his inheritance, left home, and squandered it on parties and friends. "When he had nothing left and hunger forced him to eat with the pigs, he decided to return home, if only as a hired hand, and beg for his father's mercy."

Eli didn't exactly understand what was happening, but he felt different inside. His heart had softened somehow over the last couple of months as he'd spent time here at the youth center—softened toward God. He no longer felt angry with Him, no longer blamed Him for all of the rotten stuff in his life.

The chief's voice had grown softer and a bit raspy. "While the boy was still a long way off, the father ran to him. He threw a party in his son's honor. 'My son was lost and now he's found.'" He swallowed hard. "I've been that boy, Eli. I chose what I thought was the good life." He cleared his throat. "The good life isn't women and parties. The good life is the joy and peace that come from walking in obedience and living for the Lord. And just as He did for me, He's waiting to welcome you home."

Eli could barely breathe past the wall of tears lodged in his throat. "How?" He could scarcely get anything else out. "How do I find my way home?" A single tear rolled down his cheek.

"Just talk to God like you're talking to me. Tell Him you want to accept His forgiveness for. . . name a few things that come to mind. Tell Him you want to come home."

Eli nodded.

"Would you like a few minutes alone with God?"

Again he bobbed his head, unable to speak. His throat burned.

"I'll give you about thirty minutes, and then I'll come back and we can pray together." The chief grabbed a Bible off the desk and flipped through it. He handed it open to Eli and pointed to a passage. "Here's the story if you want to read it for yourself." He quietly shut the door on his way out.

Eli hung his head and cried as he hadn't cried since Ronny's funeral. He listed the sins that came to mind in his conversation with God and asked Him to forgive them. Just as he couldn't see the wind but often felt its presence, he knew God was right there, and he experienced His love.

After he finished praying for himself and his dad, he reread the story in Luke 15. Eli understood not being worthy to be called God's son, but he also knew that because of Jesus' death on the cross, he was indeed worthy. As he read in verse twenty-four, "This son of mine was dead and is alive again; he was lost and is found." Eli knew he'd been found, and he, too, felt like celebrating.

The person he'd most like to celebrate with was Delanie, but that wouldn't work. He asked God to help him forgive his brother, his mom, his dad, and all of the other people who'd hurt and disappointed him along the way. He longed to find freedom from yesterday and freedom from his feelings for Delanie.

Chief Cooper returned and hugged Eli and then prayed

for him, asking God to grow Eli into a man of the Word, a man of prayer, and a man of integrity like Daniel. After his prayer he presented Eli with a brand-new Bible. "Start with John. And remember life is going to happen—the good, the bad, and the ugly—and through it all, God's provisions can be seen if we look for them."

"I'll remember that, sir."

The chief stopped, his hand on the door handle. "And when you're ready, I'd like you to share your testimony. Who knows? It might be just what someone else needs to hear."

Eli grinned. He felt a hundred pounds lighter. "Will you give me a couple of weeks?"

"Done."

"And, sir, will you not tell Delanie? I'd like to surprise her when I share my story." He knew he should apologize to her for crossing the line the other day.

"Deal. And welcome to the family." The chief held out his right hand.

Welcome to the family?

"The family of God."

"Oh."

"You're now my brother in Christ."

"Got it."

❧

The next morning Delanie arrived a few minutes late. Upon unlocking the office door, she found Eli humming. Humming! *What in the world?*

"Good morning." His greeting was exuberant.

" 'Morning," she said, still bleary-eyed.

"Before Mildred arrives and we have to focus solely on her, I wanted to apologize to you."

Delanie nearly dropped her coffee. She set it on the desk

and slipped her purse off her shoulder. "To me? For what?"

"I'm sorry about the other day, and it won't *ever* happen again. I was out of line."

"I'm sorry, too, Eli. I way overreacted." She forced her feet to remain planted, wanting nothing more than to run into his arms.

"Then let's forget it, okay?"

"Done." She settled at her desk, pondering what had just taken place. She booted up her computer, contemplating the change in Eli. He'd apologized, and he wasn't the apologizing type. *What gives?*

Soon both she and Eli stared into the video feed of George's empty waiting room. She laughed. "Wonder what he'd think of his nickname *Georgie*."

Eli chuckled.

Delanie sipped her coffee and waited, waited and wondered, wondered about the change in Eli.

Mildred arrived at the office about ten minutes before eight, and she, too, hummed in the morning. Delanie wondered if she'd missed out on some phenomenon that was going around. She had zero desire to hum in the morning.

A couple of hours later, a pregnant teen and her parents entered the office across the hall. Delanie glanced at Eli and he at her.

Mildred greeted them. "I'm new, so you'll have to bear with me. Is this your first visit?"

"Yes," the man answered. "Dr. Barnes sent us."

"Dr. Barnes, huh?" Mildred searched the desk. "Oh, here it is. I'll need you to fill out this intake form, and Mr. Benavides will be with you shortly."

The gentleman took the form and returned to the seat next to his wife.

Delanie• already had the phone book open. "Dr. George Barnes," she whispered. "An ob-gyn."

"Why are you whispering?" Eli asked.

She laughed. "So they don't hear me. Guess that can't happen, can it?"

"Not likely."

Eli took the phone book and found the listing. "Now the question is, how do all these young girls get connected with this doctor?"

"Another missing piece of the puzzle."

When the attorney took the clients back to his office, Mildred searched some files. Every time she found another patient of Dr. Barnes, she gave a thumbs-up. Eli kept track of Mildred's signals while Delanie listened in on the conversation back in George's private office, jotting down a few notes as they conversed.

"I think I may have found our link," she whispered. She handed Eli a piece of paper with the name of a school guidance counselor scribbled across it.

Eli acknowledged her lead and refocused on the monitor. "Shut the file cabinet." Eli coached Mildred, though she couldn't hear him. "They're coming. Mildred, they. . .are. . . coming."

Mildred must have heard them coming down the hall, because she quietly closed the cabinet and whipped out a feather duster. She smiled at George as he escorted his new clients to the door.

"You are good, woman," Eli praised her. "You are good! Quick thinker, that Mildred."

"Are there any tasks you'd like done while I'm here?" Mildred asked George when the clients left. "I thought I'd dust, but is there any typing, filing, or anything else you need?"

"No, but thanks."

"Am I doing the job all right? I'm hoping for a good reference from you to the temp agency, so I want to be certain you're pleased."

"You're doing fine." He appeared distracted. "I have a luncheon appointment. I'll be back later."

"Yes, sir."

He left the office.

"What did you learn from eavesdropping on the meeting with George?" Eli questioned.

"I'll play it back for you." Delanie hit a couple of keys on her computer and replayed the tape from a few minutes before.

A very compassionate George Benavides explained the adoption process to the family. There was no mention of money. The only headway was a doctor's name. The same referral name found in fifteen other files.

Eli phoned and updated Sarge.

Delanie spent a long afternoon watching Mildred dig through files and listening to her hum. Eli said he'd plant himself in the lobby so he could warn her when George returned. The day dragged on much as their time did watching Brandi.

Delanie phoned Joe. "How late will you be there tonight?"

"Sixish. Why?"

"I just wanted to drop in and have a chat."

"Alone?"

"Alone. I won't make it until 5:45 or so."

"I'll be here."

The day ended uneventfully, and Delanie headed straight for the department. Upon entering Joe's office, she pushed his door shut.

"One of those kinds of talks, huh?" Joe raised his eyebrow.

Delanie sat on the edge of the padded chair. "When this case ends, and it may soon, I need a new partner."

"Eli getting to you?"

"Not in the way you might think."

Joe frowned. "I'm not following."

"I'm in love with him."

"I thought so!" His face lit up, and he slapped his knee.

How could he possibly be excited?

"Not a good idea for two lovebirds to work together." He resembled the cat who swallowed the little yellow bird.

"I cannot be in love with Eli. You know what the Bible says about being unequally yoked." The sadness weighing down her heart made it feel heavy in her chest.

"I hadn't thought that far ahead." Joe rubbed his forehead with the tips of his fingers. "I guess I'd hoped, with all the time he was spending with God's people, hearing God's Word, a seed would have sprouted."

"Me, too." Delanie sighed.

"After this assignment we'll figure out something. Hey, I already called Eli, but in the morning I need you two in here instead of the bank building. I got someone else to cover Mildred. You and Eli have a doctor's appointment."

"But I'm not really pregnant. Don't you think he may figure that out?"

Joe winked. "I've got a plan, but"—he glanced at his watch—"I'm late. I'll fill you in tomorrow." He grabbed his jacket off the back of his chair and was gone.

Delanie both dreaded and ached for this case to end. The sooner the better. Maybe then her heart could start to heal. Maybe Eli's would, too.

≈

Eli arranged to meet with Sarge a half hour before Delanie's arrival time. When Eli got there, he closed the door. Sarge raised his brows but said nothing.

"When this case ends, I need a new partner."

"I thought by now you'd have figured out she's a decent cop."

"She's better than decent," Eli corrected.

"What, then? Are you still on your 'I won't work with a woman' kick?"

"Not completely, but I'd still prefer my next partner to be a man. I believe Delanie is the exception rather than the rule."

"So you respect her as a cop. What's the problem, then?"

"It's complicated," Eli said hesitantly. He'd humiliated himself enough for one lifetime and didn't want to relive it for another human being.

Sarge said nothing but gave Eli the eye as his dad used to years ago.

"All right. I'm in love with her—but it won't work. Are you satisfied?"

"When the case closes, I'll see who's available."

Not a firm promise, Eli noted. "I'd like to put in for the drug detail again."

Sarge nodded.

There was a single rap on the door. "Yo!" Sarge hollered.

Delanie entered. She glanced from one to the other. Her eyes filled with questions, such as why she'd been left out of this powwow.

Neither offered her an explanation.

A second later a pregnant woman entered. She could have been Delanie's sister—small, blond, but not nearly as pretty.

"Delanie, Eli, meet Suzy Jones, aka Lanie Lucas—for today." Delanie's gaze met his. "Eli and Lanie have a doctor's appointment in"—he checked his watch—"two hours. Turns out old Doc Barnes had a cancellation today. Delanie, you and I will attend the appointment from the parking lot, via earpiece. We can only wire Eli for obvious reasons. During the doctor's exam he might stumble across the equipment."

"Wait." Eli didn't care for the sound of this. "I'm going in with her for an examination?"

"Where's cool, calm Eli?" Delanie teased.

"We have it all figured out, and Suzy's husband gave his blessing," Sarge assured them. "It will be aboveboard. The appointment is for a consultation, so there shouldn't be an exam; but in case there is, Eli will play the squeamish boyfriend and station himself at Suzy's head. Should anything get personal, he can turn away and close his eyes."

Eli arched his brow. "And Mr. Jones isn't going to hunt me down later?" He wasn't liking this one bit.

"No, he's very mild-mannered. Anything for the force, you know." Suzy patted her slightly protruding tummy.

"How far along are you?" Delanie asked.

Eli heard a tinge of longing in her question.

"Five months. We just found out it's a little girl, which is what we hoped for. We already have a two-year-old son."

"Nice." Delanie smiled.

Eli left them to their chitchat and ran down to get a body pack. He brought back the earpieces for Sarge and Delanie.

"Let's get this show on the road." Sarge headed for the door. He led them to an SUV parked in the police lot.

❧

Delanie sat in the back with Suzy, and they talked about having a police job with a husband and kids. When Suzy and Eli went into the office building, Delanie joined Sarge in the front, claiming the passenger seat.

They listened to Eli and Suzy as they signed in and filled out forms. Since it had been discussed beforehand, Delanie knew the couple would write that Eli was unemployed and Lanie worked at the Burger House. They would check the no-insurance box. And Eli would pay with cash. Joe had every detail covered. He always did.

"Lanie Lucas," a pleasant voice called out. Delanie heard shuffling, and then the voice said, "I'll show you into the doctor's private office, where he does consults."

Delanie heard the sound of shoes against a tile floor. The same voice said, "He'll be in shortly." And then nothing. Dead silence.

After what seemed like forever, she heard a brief knock and the squeak of a door. "Lanie Lucas, I'm Dr. Barnes."

"This is my boyfriend, Ethan Farnsworth."

"Mr. Farnsworth."

Delanie could easily picture Eli's expressions.

"I see you two aren't in great financial shape to pay for this pregnancy."

"No, sir." Suzy came across as timid and unsure. "My parents aren't exactly thrilled, either. They kicked me out, so we can't count on their help."

"Have you considered adoption?"

"Bingo!" Joe said.

"Well. . ." Suzy hesitated.

"That's what I think we should do." Eli spoke up.

"You know," the doctor continued, "you can often ask for the baby's expenses to be covered by the adoptive parents, things like the doctor and hospital bill."

"How?" Suzy played the role well.

"I know a lawyer." There was a pause. "Here's his card. I'd recommend you meet with him and weigh your options."

"If we meet with him, are we committed to adoption?"

"Good job, Suze." Joe gave Delanie a thumbs-up.

"Not at all," the doctor assured her in a good-old-boy voice. "You're just checking out the possibilities, nothing more."

"I think I'd like that. At least, like the doctor said, we'd know what our choices are."

Eli's voice brought with it a pang of regret for Delanie. *How I wish we had choices.*

"Do we just call the number on this card?" he asked.

"No. The appointment has to be made through our office. He doesn't take walk-ins. If you'd like, I can have my receptionist set it up for you."

So that's how it works.

"Sure," Eli agreed.

"I don't know." Suzy was holding back.

Delanie thought they did a good job of sounding conflicted, like a true couple might.

"Remember—it's only to see what opportunities are out there for both you and your child," the doctor reminded her in a caring tone.

"Smooth, very smooth." Joe shook his head in disgust.

"Excuse me. I'll be but a moment." They heard the click of a door, so Delanie assumed the doctor had left.

The office was silent while he was gone.

"I wish they'd argue like a real couple might, in case the place is bugged, which it probably is," Joe commented amid the silence.

The door squeaked. "Mr. Benavides has an opening tomorrow morning. Why don't you at least pay him a visit and hear what he has to say?" The man's solicitous tone grated on Delanie. "He's expecting you both, and please take your picture ID."

"We're in!" Joe yelled and high-fived Delanie. "Finally."

thirteen

Delanie finished her jog and was walking her final mile to cool down. Today marked the beginning of the end. As they neared the finish line on the case, and she closed in on the termination of her partnership with Eli, she dealt with a plethora of emotions—anxiety, fear, regret, sorrow.

"God, don't let this heartache be wasted. Use it to reveal more of Yourself and to refine me. More of You, less of me." That was the constant cry of her heart, but she had such a long way to go.

Arriving at her town house, she fed her dogs and hopped in the shower. Tonight she and Courtney were meeting for dinner. Courtney thought they were discussing wedding details, but in truth Delanie planned an ambush. She'd invited a friend from high school to join them, a friend who'd married an unbeliever. She couldn't just roll over without at least trying. When Courtney was fully informed and still chose Tad, that would be her business, but Delanie decided she needed all of the facts and felt God nudging her to supply them.

She met Courtney at a restaurant in Sparks, one they hadn't been to before. She'd picked up Mickie on the way. Courtney was already seated when they arrived. Her surprise was evident when the two of them showed up.

"Courtney, this is an old friend from high school, Mickie Jordan, now Mickie Banks."

Courtney hugged Delanie and sent Mickie a smile. "I

remember you." She slid back into the circular booth. "You were one of Delanie's brainy friends."

"Guilty as charged. We were on the debate team together." Mickie adjusted her glasses.

Delanie slid into the booth first, and Mickie followed.

"Are you a wedding planner?" Courtney tried to piece the puzzle together.

Mickie giggled. "No. Sadly, I have no right brain at all. Wedding planning would debilitate me. I could never do something so creative, though I wish I could."

"Mickie is a chemical engineer." Delanie placed her napkin in her lap.

"Oh?" The question mark in Courtney's tone grew. Her gaze settled on Delanie; she obviously expected an explanation.

Delanie picked up her menu. "Let's order. I'm starving." She wanted to wait until after the waiter came, figuring Courtney would be less likely to leave if she had food on the way.

They perused the menus in silence, and when the waiter returned, they each placed their order.

"Courtney, the reason I brought Mickie tonight has nothing to do with your wedding and everything to do with your groom." Delanie paused to let the information sink in.

"What?" Courtney's gaze shifted to Mickie. "Do you know Tad?"

"No, but I'm married to a guy just like him—a guy who doesn't know God in a personal way."

Anger settled over Courtney's features, and her face reddened. Glaring at Delanie, she said, "I don't appreciate your interference. It's none of your business."

Delanie wasn't sure whether Courtney would stick around or not. Her posture indicated flight. "Courtney, please, please hear us out. I will never bring it up again, if only you will sit through this dinner with an open mind and open ears."

"Why should I?" The pulse in the side of Courtney's neck popped in and out.

"You told me I'm your oldest and dearest friend. If that's true, then you know how much I love you."

Courtney's expression softened the tiniest bit.

Delanie inhaled a deep breath. "You say this is none of my business, but as your friend and your sister in the Lord, I have to, at the very least, arm you with all the facts. I *have* to be certain you understand the reality of saying 'I do' to a man who doesn't share your faith."

"Fair enough." Courtney rearranged her silverware. "I'll listen if you promise this is the end of your crusade. From this day forward you'll accept my decision and be happy for me. You're my maid of honor, and the least you can do is share in my excitement."

Courtney was right. Delanie never should have accepted the position when she was so convinced of the wrongness of Courtney's choice. *Too late to turn back now.* "I promise." If Courtney plowed ahead, she wasn't sure how she'd feign happiness, let alone excitement, but she would do her best. Nobody wanted a dour maid of honor.

"Okay." Courtney accepted her iced tea from the waiter.

Then he placed a glass of ice water in front of Delanie and a diet soda next to Mickie's silverware.

Delanie glanced at Mickie. "You're on."

Mickie smiled at Courtney. "I'm not here to talk you out of anything. As Delanie said, she wants you to make an informed decision, so I'll share bits and pieces of my life with you. Feel free to ask me anything. I'm going to bare my soul and be honest."

Courtney nodded, squeezing lemon into her tea.

"Just so you understand, I'm crazy about my husband. He's a great guy—kind, thoughtful, generous to a fault. We have two little boys, and he's a great dad, but who will teach my little guys to be godly husbands and fathers? Who is their role model to show them what a godly man looks like?"

Mickie paused, dabbing at the corner of her eye with a napkin. "Don't get me wrong. He teaches them many wonderful things, like work ethic and integrity, but what are the chances my boys will carry their Christianity into adulthood? The hero of their lives models the message that church is for women and kids. Real men don't need God. It's hard enough to raise godly kids with two parents who love the Lord. The odds decrease by at least 50 percent with only one parent, especially if it's not a parent of the same sex."

Courtney listened, but Delanie thought her posture was defensive. This all felt so futile.

"Courtney, I know you don't want to hear this, but at least think about what I'm saying. It can be a lonely life. There's this huge emptiness."

The waiter brought their salads.

"I hear what you're saying, but Tad does go to church. I'm sure it's just a matter of time. . ." Courtney stirred her tea.

"I meet with a group of women in the same boat. A lot of their husbands went to church for a while and then grew tired of it. Now those women go alone."

Delanie spoke up. "Courtney, most men will do anything in the wooing process, but when the honeymoon is over and reality settles in, people change."

"She's right," Mickie said. "I'm reading a book titled *Spiritually Single*. Why don't you at least read it before the wedding? The author is crazy about her husband, but she faced a long and lonely trek for many years. It will give you an idea of what you might face in the days and years ahead."

"I'll think about it." Courtney studied Mickie. "Tell me something—would you marry him all over again?"

Mickie sighed. "That's a really hard question. I love him. We have history and children. Do I relish the spiritual loneliness? No. Do I love the man? With all my heart. If I knew then what I know now, I'd never have said yes to the first date."

"But I already said yes—to the first date, to falling in love, and to his proposal. I think I'm in too deep to turn back now."

Now it was Courtney's turn to dab her eyes. Delanie joined her.

"It's not too late until you've signed the license." Mickie gave Courtney's hand a squeeze.

"Sometimes I am afraid." Courtney's gaze shifted from one to the other. "And I wonder if I'm making the biggest mistake of my life, but it's too late." Courtney paused and swallowed hard. "I've given too much of myself, my heart and other things that I can't get back. I won't change my mind now."

A deep sorrow settled over Delanie. She'd tried and failed. For better or for worse, Courtney would yoke herself to Tad.

Mickie also seemed to sense the futility of their mission. She said nothing more. They shifted into small talk and finished their meal. Delanie prayed she could keep her promise. Her emotions were at the opposite end of the spectrum from happy and excited. Even worse, she sensed Courtney's were, as well.

❧

"Months of hard work are coming to an end," Eli announced

in Sarge's office the next morning.

"It feels good, doesn't it?" Sarge glanced up from the folder of paperwork. "This is what we live for—the bust. Beating criminals at their own game and sending men who think they're above the law up the river for a very long time."

"You sound positively thrilled." Delanie grinned.

"I am. I hate people who think they can do as they please with no personal cost. These men have gotten very rich preying on young girls and poor families. Nothing will make me happier than seeing them behind bars. Adding murder to the mix only increases the length of their stay."

Delanie sighed. "If only it were that easy, that cut-and-dried. Sadly, we all know this is just the beginning."

"Now we hope for a jury to see things our way." Eli finished cleaning his gun and returned it to the holster under his pant leg. Then he retrieved the pistol from under his arm. His heart beat faster in anticipation. He, like Sarge, lived for this moment. The bust made the hours of boring stakeouts worth it.

He no longer feared being partnered with Delanie, not in light of her skill and ability on the job. He did, however, fear the damage she'd done to his heart. He knew she wanted another partner as much as he did, so if they made an arrest today, this could end up being their last day together.

The thought brought mixed feelings—sorrow and relief. Nevertheless, he'd see her around. She wouldn't avoid the youth center forever, though a part of him wished she would. He was sure running into her in the future would be a mixed bag.

What he dreaded was the day he ran into her with another guy or the day he heard she was marrying someone else. Eli sighed and checked his chamber. *Time heals all wounds.* Eli knew from personal experience God healed better than time did. He'd made more progress in the past week than in the past two decades.

Smiling, he wondered how Delanie might react when she finally heard his testimony. Her dad promised he'd get her to the center on Saturday. For some reason it was important to Eli that she hear his story, that she know her prayers made a difference. If not for Delanie, he doubted he ever would have given God a second chance. He supposed his unrequited love was worth that.

"Everything's in order." Sarge fanned through the stack of forms one last time. "The warrants are secured." He stood the pile on end and tapped it against his desk, aligning the edges just so. "Months of tailing pregnant girls, attempting interviews with possible adoptive couples, and staking out law firm after law firm ends in this." Sarge waved the folder filled with the evidence, case notes, and legal documents they'd collected. "Soon this will all be passed to the DA, and whether he wins or loses has a lot to do with how well we did our job and the written substantiation we provide. Once we tie them to the baby-selling ring, we're hoping their own files will tie them to the murder victims."

Eli admired Sarge's work ethic; he wanted everything done right and well. He didn't just want the arrest; he went after the conviction.

"The sad thing about that file folder—it's only paper." Delanie's gloomy gaze connected with Eli's. "We've met the people and seen how their lives were affected. Brandi wasn't just a death certificate, a picture, or an autopsy report; she was a flesh-and-blood person who mattered to somebody. And her baby mattered. My hope is that the doctor and the lawyer who run this baby-selling ring are both prosecuted to the full extent of the law."

"We're all on the same page," Sarge assured her. "You're preaching to the choir."

Eli glanced at his watch. "It's about time to roll." He and Delanie both had their wires on, and with her fake belly, they looked very much the part of young expectant parents. A part he'd never play in real life...

Sarge stationed a couple of men across the hall, just in case, though nobody expected more than a routine arrest. "You two be careful. Play it cool, but play it safe."

They both gave Sarge a nod and headed for the car. Eli drove the few blocks to downtown, pulling into the parking garage. Before leaving the car, they double-checked all of their equipment, including their guns. This time there would be no tender scene, no crazy unreturned proclamations—just two cops doing their jobs.

Delanie was quiet and kept clasping and unclasping her hands. Eli figured their nervousness would work to their advantage, which wouldn't be the case in a drug deal. He assumed a young couple considering selling their baby might be a little uneasy.

He held open the door, and Delanie waddled through. She always walked funny with the big belly strapped to her. He'd bet she sure would be cute pregnant. The second he caught the direction of his thoughts, he refocused on the case.

The elevator doors opened, and they stepped inside. Delanie closed her eyes, and he assumed she was praying. He shot up a quick prayer himself. He'd been in much more dangerous situations than this. No one in their right mind would resist arrest in an office complex, filled with people, in broad daylight. Old Georgie's chances would be much greater if he hired a good attorney rather than put up a fight.

They left the elevator and strolled down the hall to the

correct office. At least he knew he could count on Delanie—that felt good.

He opened the office door, and she entered first. She approached Mildred's desk. "We're here for our appointment. Lanie Lucas and Ethan—"

"Yes, your paperwork was faxed over this morning." No one would ever guess Mildred knew them or they her. There were no conspiratorial glances or words exchanged with hidden meaning.

Delanie picked up a magazine and took the chair next to Eli's. "I'm not sure this is the right choice," she whispered.

Eli caught a glimpse of a man at the edge of the doorway. They'd put on a good show for him. "Lanie, I don't know what else to do. I have no job. Your parents kicked you out. My old lady isn't going to let us live with her forever."

"But this is our baby." She laid her hand over her padded protrusion. "This is you and me—a consummation of our love. How can you just give our child to a stranger?"

"Love is doing the selfless thing. We have the opportunity to give this baby more—so much more—by letting a wealthy family adopt it and raise it."

"He's not an it!" Delanie raised her voice. "He's a baby. I hate when you do that."

The shoes Eli had seen on the man in the hall stepped around the corner. "Lanie Lucas and Ethan Farnsworth?"

"Yes," they answered in unison.

The man in the expensive suit held out his hand. "I'm George Benavides." Eli shook the guy's hand. "Would you please follow me back to my private office?"

Not as private as you think, buddy. We've got people listening.

Georgie led them and once inside waved his hand toward two leather chairs facing his desk. The desk was fashioned from dark wood, a beautiful piece of furniture—large and masculine.

"Dr. Barnes said you'd like to hear the options. Of course, please understand you're under no obligation. I'm only here to present to you other alternatives than raising your own child. Why might adoption appeal to you?" He raised his brows, his gaze bouncing back and forth from him to Delanie.

Eli knew the guy had already heard the list of reasons he'd verbalized to Delanie while they waited in the reception area. He'd been eavesdropping, but to appease the man, Eli recited them again.

"You make some good points. A few other considerations"—his gaze focused on Delanie—"the child's education. People who spend thousands of dollars on a baby aren't likely to settle for public school. These are highly intelligent individuals, and for any offspring of theirs to receive less than a college degree is unheard of. You get to choose the parents you want for your little one." He laid out several résumés of couples waiting for a baby. "These are all wealthy professionals, and your infant would have the best of everything."

"But would a stranger love our newborn the way we would?" Delanie understood a mother's heart.

Georgie put on his most compassionate face and patted her hand. "Sometimes more, dear, sometimes more. Think of their heartbreak. Many have struggled to produce an heir for over a decade. Sometimes the longer a person waits and the more they want something, the more likely they are to appreciate the culmination of their dreams."

Delanie bit her bottom lip and picked up one of the résumés.

"Dr. Barnes said all our expenses would be covered." She raised her gaze from the paperwork.

He nodded. "That's true. Though it's illegal to sell a child, it is acceptable to cover the medical expenses accrued."

What game did Georgie-boy play? Maybe he kept the proceeds for himself. Eli decided to push. Without an offer of money, they had nothing.

"A guy down at the bar—"

"What bar?" Not a trusting soul, this Georgie-boy.

Eli rattled off the name of a corner joint not far from his place. "Anyway, he said his sister and brother-in-law made twenty thousand dollars for their baby. Said he could hook me up."

"As I said, that is illegal."

Eli nodded and looked the guy over. "I promised Lanie here that if we gave up the baby, we'd have some dough to start fresh, buy her some nice things." He rose. "I think I'll see if Jose can hook us up with the guy his sister used."

George studied them. Delanie rose, glancing from him to Eli. He reached for her hand, and they took their first step toward the door.

"Wait."

They paused.

"Twenty thousand?"

Eli nodded but didn't return to his chair.

Delanie whispered, "This isn't working out. I think it's a sign we should keep the baby."

"Please take your seats for another moment." George motioned them back. They complied.

"Are you willing to sign a contract today if I can get you twenty thousand dollars?"

Eli was quick to agree. Delanie held out.

George pulled a contract from his drawer. "I'll get you the twenty thousand if you agree to silence. Baby selling is a class

B felony—enough to get you a lengthy stay in the pen."

How clever of him to manipulate the parents into shouldering the blame. No wonder they couldn't find a single person to rat him out. He had them convinced that they did the crime and they'd do the time. Somehow he managed to come off seeming like the hero.

Delanie looked at Eli. "That's a lot of money."

"It is, baby; it is. We could get a place to live, a decent set of wheels. . ."

Delanie pulled her lips together in a tight line and cradled her belly. A tiny tear escaped the corner of her eye.

"How about twenty-five thousand?" George dangled a bigger carrot.

Her mouth dropped open. She glanced at Eli, and he gave her a nod. She stared down at her stomach. Sucking in a big breath, she said, "Okay." She turned her attention to George. "We'll do it."

The attorney filled in the blanks with an ink pen on a premade form. Interesting that a guy who didn't regularly pay people for babies had a contract all drawn up and ready to sign.

While Eli examined the contract, he noticed George scrutinizing Delanie for about the tenth time.

"You look very familiar to me." George drew his brows together. "I never forget a face. Are you friends with one of my kids?"

Delanie shook her head. "I don't think so."

"Where do you go to high school?" he demanded.

Delanie froze, and Eli knew she'd forgotten the name of the school they'd discussed. His heart beat faster. *Say something, Delanie; say anything.* Though only seconds ticked by, for Eli it felt like days.

She named the high school she'd graduated from.

Eli watched the attorney's demeanor and expression change. Somehow he knew. He knew!

He grabbed the signed contract with Eli's still damp signature. "If you'll excuse me, I'll have Mildred make copies."

Eli grabbed Delanie's hand and squeezed. When she made eye contact, he mouthed the words *"He knows."*

fourteen

Mildred shouted from the hall. "He left! He left the office!"

Eli and Delanie were on their feet and at a dead run. They paused in the hall. He looked left. She took off full speed to the right. Eli followed, and the two officers in the faux office across the hall were dead on his heels.

Delanie tugged open the stairwell door. She was fast; he'd only now caught up to her.

"Did you see him take the stairs?" Eli shouted.

"Yes."

He paused. "You guys go up. We'll go down."

Delanie was already at the bottom of the first half of the flight of stairs. She rounded a corner, and he lost sight of her. Panic spurred him to move even faster. *God, keep her safe.* When he got to the second floor she was still about a quarter of a flight ahead of him.

When she disappeared around the next bend, he heard her yell, "Freeze!" And his heart did just that. Fear for her safety fell over him like a blanket, nearly suffocating him. Circling the next turn, he almost collided with Delanie. He was thankful he didn't. He'd have knocked her gun out of her hand, and they'd have been at George's mercy. As it was now, all three of them held weapons. He and Delanie had the advantage because there were two of them.

Eli decided to stall until their backup arrived. It could take them awhile to follow the stairwell to the roof and back down again once they discovered their assailant went the other direction. "What tipped you off, George?" Eli was surprised by how calm his voice sounded, because inside him was turbulence.

"Her." He took a step backward and moved down one stair.

Eli followed suit, feeling better with Delanie behind him.

"Don't come any closer." George raised his gun.

"George, you're fighting a lost cause. Other patrolmen are on their way. You don't stand a chance." The man had a wild look in his eyes, one Eli had seen before. George wasn't in a surrendering mood. Eli took another step, and Delanie did the same. She stood one step higher and to his right. Her gun was level with his ear.

"Don't move again." George was panicked. He had that fight-or-flight expression. "I'll shoot her if either of you moves again."

Dear God, please, no. "We won't move, George. Will we, Cooper?"

"No." Her breathing was rapid.

He heard the other officers running down the stairs. How he wished they were apprised of the situation. He braced himself for a possible crash when they rounded the corner.

"George!" Eli yelled. "Give yourself up."

The running stopped. A stairwell door opened and shut. *They heard me.* They'd get to the first floor and come in from behind.

George raised his gun. "I won't go down alone."

Eli stepped in front of Delanie, but she shifted to the other side of the stairwell. Not what he'd intended.

The door behind George creaked, and Eli's gaze shifted for a mere second from the assailant to their backup. Delanie leapt in front of him. She yelled, "No!" Her gun fired at the same time he saw a flash from George's. The noise from the two shots echoed through the stairwell with deafening certainty. One of the bullets ricocheted off the metal stair rail. Delanie fell back against him. George crumpled to the ground.

Eli lowered himself onto the stair, gently cradling Delanie. His left hand that lay just under her rib cage was wet and gooey, covered in her blood. "Oh, dear God, please help her."

"Officer down! I repeat, officer down." One of the two patrolmen knelt over George's still form. The other yelled into his radio. "Shots fired! Send an ambulance! Now!"

Eli sat very still, trying to support her without moving. She was losing blood at a steady rate.

"Please don't die," he whispered. It took all his willpower not to sob.

Delanie opened her dazed eyes. "I'm. . .sorry. So. . .very. . . sorry."

"Shh." He caressed her cheek. "You have nothing to be sorry for. You're the bravest person I've ever known."

She moved her head to the side. "My. . .fault. Sorry."

Breathing seemed increasingly difficult for Delanie. "Where are the paramedics?" Eli asked in a loud whisper.

"On their way," the other officer promised. He had joined Eli and was leaning over Delanie.

"Hang tough, Delanie. They're almost here. You'll be fine." How Eli wished he truly believed his own words.

"Forgive. . .me?" Her eyes were glazed over. "Let. . .you. . . down."

"No." He fought the tears. He must be brave for her.

"E?" She gasped for breath.

"I'm right here." He stroked her hair.

"Love. . .you. . .t. . ." Her body went limp in his arms.

"Get somebody here now!" *Dear God, please don't let her die. Please.*

The paramedics ran up the stairs, carrying a gurney. Eli moved out of their way.

"She's in respiratory arrest with a weak and thready pulse." The words nearly stopped Eli's heart.

"Bag her."

They slipped a mask over Delanie's face and squeezed an air bag, letting the air flow in and out. The paramedic literally breathed for her with his hands.

"Let's go. We need to get her in."

"Will she be all right?" *Please say yes.*

"It's touch and go. She's lost a lot of blood." They carefully lifted her to the stretcher. "We've got to get her to the ER. She needs a chest tube inserted." They strapped her down and wheeled her out. Eli followed until Sarge grabbed his arm.

"Come with me. They're taking her to St. Mary's. I'll give you a ride."

The ambulance shot out from the drive in front of the building, the siren screeching.

"She may not make it." Tears ran down Eli's cheeks. "They said touch and go."

Sarge put his big hand on Eli's shoulder. "Pray. It's our best option."

Never has been for me. He hated feeling that way. Then he echoed a prayer he'd read recently in his Bible. *Lord, help my unbelief.*

"She said she loved me. Do you think she meant it?" Eli watched the ambulance until it disappeared from his sight.

"She did," Sarge assured him without hesitation. "I can guarantee she did."

When they arrived at the ER, Chief Cooper was already there, his face ashen. Eli wondered if her dad would hate him for not protecting Delanie better.

"Eli, Joe." Chief Cooper came over and gave both men a hug. "They've taken her in to insert two chest tubes. I got here before the ambulance arrived. I caught a glimpse of her. She looks bad." His shoulders sagged. "What they know at this point is that she has hemothorax and pneumothorax, both the result of a collapsed lung."

"What does that mean?" Sarge asked.

"She has blood and air in her chest cavity due to the bullet wound and the nonfunctioning lung. The chest tubes will reinflate the lung. Once that's done and she stabilizes, they'll take her to surgery and remove the bullet."

Marilyn Cooper, a woman not much bigger than her daughter, rushed through the sliding doors and straight into the chief's arms. Once in his embrace, she wept uncontrollably.

Eli decided to give them some space. "I think I'll find the chapel."

"I'll join you." Sarge followed.

"I'm terrified she's going to die." He whispered his greatest fear as they followed the signs to the hospital chapel.

"Me, too." Sarge's voice broke. "It's this way." He veered right. "I was here almost a year ago, praying for you while you were in surgery."

The news touched Eli. "Thank you." He patted the big guy's back. Then his thoughts returned to Delanie. "I was so wrong about her." He settled into one of the blue padded chairs and rested his head in his hands. "I was afraid I'd have to take a bullet for her. I never guessed she'd take one for me."

"What happened?"

Eli focused on the stained-glass window at the front of the room. "She was behind me on the steps. When she saw him aim the gun, she jumped in front of me and fired."

"Sounds intentional."

"She was protecting me." He stood, running his hands through his hair. "I should have been the one protecting her. Then she apologized for letting me down, but the entire fault is mine. When I heard the door open, I shifted my gaze for a split second. He'd have shot me, and I never would have seen it coming." He returned to his chair. "Maybe if I hadn't been so hard on her in the beginning, she wouldn't have felt the need to prove herself."

"Eli, sometimes heroics are instinctual. This isn't the first time Delanie's risked her life for the job. Probably would have been her gut reaction no matter how you treated her early on."

"You think?" He wanted to grab hold of that idea and believe it with all his heart.

"I know, and I also know she thought you were pretty terrific."

Eli didn't feel terrific. All he knew was, given the chance, he'd go back and do it all differently, everything except loving her.

"Why do you believe that when Delanie said she loved me she meant it?"

"When people face death, that's when they are the most honest."

Eli supposed Sarge was right. They spent some time in prayer together. It was Eli's first time to pray aloud in front of another person, but it came much easier than he thought it would.

When they finished, Sarge gazed at him through squinted eyes. "I didn't realize you'd become a man of faith."

"Just happened last week. I haven't even told Delanie yet—wanted to surprise her. The chief asked me to share my story at the center tomorrow. Now she may never know. . . ."

"She'll know, Eli. Whatever happens, she'll know." Sarge rose. "Let's go see if there's an update."

The prayer time calmed Eli. In the midst of it he'd come to terms with God's right to choose Delanie's future. He concluded that whatever happened, he'd survive it with God. This time he'd fight for his faith, not walk away from it. But his continual plea was a second chance to share his newfound faith with Delanie. The changes brewing within sometimes surprised him.

Back in the ER waiting room, Delanie's family huddled together in a cluster of chairs, talking in soft tones. Eli hung back, feeling like an intruder. Sarge moved in and took a seat next to her brother Cody. "Any word?"

The chief searched the area and, when he spotted Eli, motioned for him to join them. He took the chair next to Chief Cooper. Eli had met the whole family at one time or another at the center. They all welcomed him now with compassionate looks or nods. No one seemed to blame him—no one except himself. Delanie had a great team rooting for her.

"Delanie is in surgery. God was with our girl today." The chief's voice was deep and raspy. "They say the bullet must have ricocheted rather than a dead-on shot and then entered low in her chest, hit and broke a rib before lodging against a posterior rib, just above her diaphragm. It's the best-case scenario for a gunshot to the chest. That was God's protection. The doctor said if she'd been one step lower, chances are the bullet would have hit her heart for sure."

Eli liked the way this family looked at life. He'd learned much from the whole brood. Before, instead of seeing the blessing, he'd have been mad that God let it happen. Through the teaching and testimonies at the center, he'd learned that what he'd wanted before was a fairy godmother as opposed to a sovereign Lord. He'd wanted to call the shots and wanted God to do the work, his way.

When the doctor came out a couple of hours later, everyone jumped up and surrounded him.

"We got the bullet and stopped the bleeding. No major vessels were hit. Your daughter must have a guardian angel, because the damage was minimal, considering."

God again! Eli decided their thinking was contagious, and he'd caught it.

"Don't get me wrong—she's still listed in critical condition." The doctor looked around at the group that had gathered. "But from a medical standpoint, the fact that she's alive is amazing."

The doctor's words gave Eli hope.

"You may go back two at a time. But let me warn you— she's hooked up to a lot of monitors and machines. Don't let them frighten you. She's yet to regain consciousness, so don't expect a personal greeting. One last thing—she lost a lot of blood and is white as a ghost. Expect it—it's normal at this point."

The doctor led Delanie's parents into the intensive care unit. Eli realized he probably wouldn't get to go back. The sign said immediate family only; he should just pack it up and go home, but he couldn't bear to leave. Somehow he felt closer to her here.

About fifteen minutes later, her parents returned. They filled everyone in on how she looked and reiterated what they should all expect.

Eli still wrestled with what he should do. Should he stay? Should he go? He really didn't belong here. He wasn't family, and as of late he and Delanie weren't even friends.

He approached the chief. "I, uh. . .should go."

"Don't you at least want to see her first?" The chief's brows shot up.

Eli pointed. "The sign says immediate family only."

Her dad smiled and placed his hand on Eli's shoulder. "You are family. You're my spiritual son, and we're all brothers and sisters in the Lord. But more than that, Delanie would want you here. You're her partner and her friend." He gave Eli's shoulder a squeeze. "I thought Cody and Brady could go in next, then you and Sarge."

"Thank you." Surprised by how much the small gesture touched him, he felt as if he finally belonged somewhere, and belonging was a good feeling.

At the top of the next hour, her brothers went in for their short time with Delanie.

When they returned, Chief Cooper gathered everyone in a huddle. "I thought after we've each seen her for a few minutes we could take shifts sitting with her." He'd slipped into his cop persona, taking charge and having a plan. "Since there are eight of us, maybe each of us could take a three-hour segment over the next twenty-four-hour period. Of course we can only sit with her for the fifteen-minute stint at the start of each hour." Her dad glanced at Eli. "But only if each of you wants to—feel absolutely no obligation." All of them agreed they wanted their names added to the roster. Eli took the 3:00 to 6:00 a.m. time slot, leaving the better hours for her family.

A couple of hours later, he and Sarge finally got their turn and went back to Delanie's room. Eli stopped in the doorway, unprepared to see her so vulnerable. She lay there so small and fragile among all of the tubes and machines. Her skin tone gave the white sheets competition as to which was paler.

Sarge picked the chair on the far side of the bed. He laid his hand on Delanie's and hung his head. Eli knew he was praying

Gaining a new sense of purpose, Eli settled in the other chair on the opposite side of her bed. Resting his forehead against the rail of her bed, he carefully laid his hand on her arm. Her skin was cool against his fingers. He, too, beseeched God on Delanie's behalf.

A little beep on Sarge's watch indicated their time was over, and he rose and stretched. The day had now worn into evening, but Eli wasn't ready to leave yet. "Do you mind if I take an extra minute with her?"

"Go ahead. I'll be in the waiting room."

Eli stood next to her head and leaned in near her ear. "Delanie," he whispered in a shaky voice. "I've invited Jesus to be part of my life. I wanted to surprise you tomorrow with my testimony, but they say you'll be busy tomorrow. So I absolutely had to tell you—I know your Jesus." He longed to say so much more, but the last time he'd bared his feelings to her, she hadn't wanted to hear.

He touched her cheek with the tips of his fingers and decided he'd say it anyway. She'd never know. "I love you, Delanie Cooper." His tears returned. One dropped onto her pillow. He bent over and kissed her cheek. "And I know you don't feel the same way about me, but I needed to say it out loud, just this one time. My life has radically changed— thanks to God and you." He forced himself to walk away, but just before he did, he kissed the tips of his fingers and tenderly touched her lips.

When Eli returned to the waiting room, Delanie's brothers talked him into a game of Battleship. Eli was grateful he'd been invited right into the midst of things. He'd take whatever they gave him, hungry for this type of connection and acceptance.

When the game ended, Eli was tired. He tried to get comfortable in the vinyl padded chairs to grab a catnap, but it wasn't happening. Many of the guys on the force came by, as well as the volunteers from the center and many people from the Coopers' church.

People cared about this family. A woman named Valerie carried in a hot meal. Guys from Brady's paramedic unit brought sleeping bags and pillows. Eli was awed by all of the activity. He was seeing firsthand how the body of Christ functioned when one of its members was in crisis.

Eli, Cody, and Brady each grabbed a sleeping bag from the pile in the corner and unrolled them against a wall, out of the way. It felt good to stretch out his exhausted body. He hadn't realized how tired or hungry he'd been until these good people showed up with precisely what he needed.

The mood had lightened some. Clusters of folks chatted quietly. Eli shut his eyes, convinced he'd never sleep in the controlled chaos, but he did catch a few winks. When he awoke, the waiting room had emptied out. He still had several hours until his shift with Delanie. Her family and another, whose grandfather had undergone a heart attack, had taken over the alcove designated as the ICU waiting room.

Eli paced, went to the chapel for a while, then headed to the cafeteria for coffee. Time dragged. Finally, 3:00 a.m. rolled around. He headed for the double doors of the unit and made a beeline to the third door on the right. He thought Delanie's color had improved slightly.

A nurse came in and checked one of the machines, pushed a couple of buttons, and wrote something on Delanie's chart. Eli settled into the same chair he had before. Less medical equipment was on that side. He carefully slid her limp hand into his and talked to her for the next fifteen minutes. The doctor said touch and familiar voices were an important part of recovery.

They all rotated shifts over the next day and a half. As her vitals stabilized, family members began to leave for showers and sleep. Eli had gone home for a few hours to clean up and sleep in a real bed. Just as he finished his shower, his cell phone rang. His heart dropped as he read the name across the face of his phone. It was Brady.

"Hey." Eli's heart pounded hard against his ribs.

"She's awake!" Brady's voice danced over the line.

fifteen

"Thank You, Lord. Thank You!" Eli's eyes misted.

"She's asking for you."

"For me?" Someone must have misunderstood what she said.

"Yeah, man, for you." Brady chuckled over the line.

Eli's heart took flight. "I'll be right there."

"She's awake, Dad!" He grabbed hold of his dad—who'd just sauntered into the kitchen for a bite to eat before heading back to his favorite stool at the corner pub just blocks away—and hugged him as he hadn't done in years. "She's awake!"

When he arrived at the hospital not fifteen minutes later, his hair was still wet. He'd grabbed a shirt and his soccer sandals and run out of the house, forgetting the need for incidentals like warm shoes and a jacket.

Parking his car, he ran to the front entrance and took the stairs two at a time, not having the patience to wait on the elevator.

Chief Cooper was in the hall, beaming. "She seems fine. They'll do further testing on her cognitive skills, but I don't think they'll find a problem. Our God is an awesome God!"

"That He is. Is it all right if I go on in?"

The chief slapped him on the back. "Absolutely."

Eli stopped in the doorway. They had rolled the head of her bed up some so she was halfway between lying and sitting. Her eyes were closed, and though still pale, she had much more color than yesterday morning. The doc had said the transfusion would do that. His heart felt as though it might burst at the seams; he was so full of love for her.

Standing there, he suddenly felt shy. He'd said a lot of things to her since the shooting. What if she remembered? His face grew warm at the thought.

She opened her eyes, and he was certain they brightened when she saw him. "Eli, you came." Her voice was soft and weak.

He moved to her bed. "Of course I came."

"I'm so sorry I botched the case. How did I blow our cover?"

"Turns out they were only targeting a couple of the poorer high schools in the city. Dr. Barnes had met with a few of the guidance counselors, generously offering his free prenatal care to pregnant teens desiring to keep their babies or those planning to put them up for adoption. None of the high school employees knew what he was really up to."

"The baby-selling charges are rock solid and should be an easy conviction. The murder charges may be harder to prove, but the DA is hoping, with the help of DNA and both guys' files, to build a solid case."

Delanie moved her head in a rather weak and pathetic nod. "So when I named my high school. . ."

"He'd also seen the newspaper article about your heroics several years ago. The one with your picture—says he never forgets a face. When you named your high school, it all came together for him."

"So George isn't dead?"

"No."

❧

"I'm glad." Remembering the horrific emotions she'd dealt with after the last shooting, she was thankful to avoid that again. "I'm sorry, Eli. I nearly got one or both of us killed. My pride in my ability as a cop had a hole shot right through it."

He smiled at her pun. "It was my fault. I took my eyes off him."

"Please don't blame yourself. Guess I'm another female partner you'll say good riddance to."

He swallowed hard and shook his head. "Sarge put me back on drug detail, after a week of forced vacation. He insists I need the R & R."

A part of her wanted to cry at his news. "So the days of the dynamic duo are over. I don't guess I'll be on active duty anytime soon."

"Probably not." His mood was solemn.

Delanie's eyes filled with tears. "So this is good-bye?"

"I'll see you around." He attempted to be chipper but fell flat. "I have so many things I want to say to you." His gaze shifted to the floor. "I'm sorry I was such a jerk to you in the beginning. I was wrong about you." He raised his gaze to meet hers. "You're a great cop—one of the best partners I've ever had."

"Right up there with Gus?"

"Yep." He smiled. "Seriously, I can't begin to list what your friendship has meant to me." His voice cracked. "And the ways God has used you in my life."

"God? Did you say God?" *Dare I hope?*

"I did say God. Your dad prayed with me last week. This prodigal quit running and found his way home."

"Oh, Eli." He blurred in her vision as her eyes teared up. She held out her hand to him, and he took it. "Last week? Why didn't you tell me?"

"I planned to this morning at the center. Your dad scheduled me to share my testimony, only you were a no-show."

"Sorry about that." She drank in every detail of his face. "I can't tell you how happy I am."

"You have a funny way of showing it." Eli pulled a tissue from the box with his free hand and dried her cheeks.

"You *are* the sweetest man." The words came out husky-sounding. Dare she tell him how she felt? Her heart raced. What if he'd changed his mind? Life was precarious at best. She had no idea what even the next minute held, so she decided not to waste it.

"Eli." She moistened her dry lips. "I love you."

❧

The words warmed his heart. "I know." He'd figured out that much about being a Christian. They all loved each other in the Lord. "I love you, too." *More than you'll ever know.* "Even though we'll probably lose touch after time"—*After you fall for some other guy*—"I'll always consider you one of my dearest friends."

"Thank you." Her smile was weak, and he knew she needed rest. "But—"

"I've worn you out and had better go—"

She tightened her grip on his hand. "Eli, stop talking." Her eyes gazed into his. "I'm *in* love with you."

He replayed her words, and his chest filled with a warm puddle in the spot previously occupied by his heart. "But I thought—"

"Don't think." She stroked his hand and smiled. "I fell in love with you hard and fast, starting the very first day."

"You mean when I was Mr. Charming? How could you have fallen for me then?"

"Seeing you with the guys from your hood blew your hard-edged image away, clinching it for me."

"Then why—"

She explained her reasons and why she didn't feel at liberty to reveal her heart to him.

"I understand." He ran his thumb across her cheek.

"So—what about you?" At his perplexed expression, she continued, "Do you still have feelings for me?"

"So many—respect, admiration, but love is at the very top of the list. I love you, Delanie Cooper."

"And I love you, Eli Logan." She tugged him closer. "Now will you kiss me, already?"

And he did. The first of a lifetime's worth.

epilogue

A year had passed since Eli had made things right with God. To commemorate his one-year birthday as a Christ follower, he would marry the love of his life.

Delanie wanted to wait a year, make sure they knew the ugly side of each other. The truth was, he hadn't found an ugly side to her, but she insisted there was one. He had yet to see it, though. Of course, love was said to be blind. And he was glad of that, because she seemed quite clueless to his flaws, as well.

Eli followed the minister up on the platform. Sarge stood next to him as his best man. He was the perfect choice; after all, he'd paired them together in the first place. As Eli stood before a church filled with people who loved them and people they loved, he anticipated his beautiful bride walking down the aisle toward him. He smiled at his dad on the first row and at each of his now high school crew lining the entire family pew.

Eli shot off a prayer for his dad. He'd finally agreed to try a rehab the chief had recommended—a Christian-based one. Eli knew firsthand God could change people from the inside out, even when several other programs had failed. They'd also train him to live on his own again. He'd stay at the old apartment, and Eli would move in with Delanie, Hank, and Junie. Of course he'd be at his dad's often, keeping an eye on him and his boys. As hard as it was to watch him continue his battle with alcoholism, Eli knew he had to give up worrying about his dad and trust that God was in control.

And he'd learned that God really was in control, even when life seemed to spin out of control.

The music began, and Frank Jr. escorted his mother down the aisle. A tinge of regret hit Eli as he thought of his own mom. As a cop, he could probably track her down, but she apparently didn't want to be found. He'd forgiven her for disappearing, and now he prayed regularly for her. Maybe someday. . .

Mason and Summer, Delanie's nephew and niece, started down the aisle. Courtney and Brady followed them. Next were Jodi and Cody, and behind them were Kristen and Frankie. Delanie couldn't choose one from among her friends, so she'd asked Sunnie, Frankie's wife, to be her matron of honor. She put the others in alphabetical order, avoiding any sort of favoritism. That was his Delanie.

As he watched them coming toward him, he noted a sadness in Courtney's eyes and a droop to her shoulders. Tad couldn't make it today. Duty called at the hospital. He'd all but quit coming to church, and their wedded bliss had already vanished. Courtney never voiced it, but both he and Delanie believed she'd grown to regret her decision. They both prayed for them regularly. If God could soften Eli, He could soften anyone.

When Sunnie reached the stage, the music changed. The "Bridal March" began. Eli's heart shifted into high gear. Delanie moved toward him on the arm of her dad. Their gazes locked. All praise and thanks to God, she'd fully recovered. As she glided closer, he knew one lifetime with her would never be enough.

"Who gives this woman?" the pastor asked when they reached the front of the church.

"Her mother and I." In many ways Frank Cooper had

become the dad to Eli that his real father had never been able to be.

"I love you, Daddy." Eli heard her whispered words.

"And I love you." He turned her veil back, kissing her cheek. "Both of you." He hugged Eli and whispered, "I'm so glad her heart found you and yours found Christ."

"Me, too." Eli had grown to love her whole wonderful family. They'd welcomed him and become all he'd ached for as a child. Not only had they embraced him, but they'd also done the same with his group of guys, including them in their gatherings.

Delanie's father placed her hand in Eli's and took his seat on the pew next to her mother. And today Delanie, this woman he cherished more than life itself, would become his wife. God had freed him from the pain of yesterday, and his tomorrows had never looked brighter.

A Letter To Our Readers

Dear Reader:

In order that we might better contribute to your reading enjoyment, we would appreciate your taking a few minutes to respond to the following questions. We welcome your comments and read each form and letter we receive. When completed, please return to the following:

Fiction Editor
Heartsong Presents
PO Box 719
Uhrichsville, Ohio 44683

1. Did you enjoy reading *Always Yesterday* by Jeri Odell?
   ❏ Very much! I would like to see more books by this author!
   ❏ Moderately. I would have enjoyed it more if

   _____

   _____

   _____

2. Are you a member of **Heartsong Presents**?   ❏ Yes   ❏ No
   If no, where did you purchase this book? _____

   _____

3. How would you rate, on a scale from 1 (poor) to 5 (superior), the cover design? _____

4. On a scale from 1 (poor) to 10 (superior), please rate the following elements.

   _____ Heroine   _____ Plot
   _____ Hero   _____ Inspirational theme
   _____ Setting   _____ Secondary characters

5. These characters were special because? _____

_____

_____

6. How has this book inspired your life? _____

_____

_____

7. What settings would you like to see covered in future
   Heartsong Presents books? _____

_____

_____

8. What are some inspirational themes you would like to see
   treated in future books? _____

_____

_____

9. Would you be interested in reading other **Heartsong
   Presents** titles? ❏ Yes ❏ No

10. Please check your age range:
    ❏ Under 18   ❏ 18-24
    ❏ 25-34   ❏ 35-45
    ❏ 46-55   ❏ Over 55

Name _____

Occupation _____

Address _____

City, State, Zip_____

Heart♥ng

Any 12 Heartsong Presents titles for only $27.00*

CONTEMPORARY ROMANCE IS CHEAPER BY THE DOZEN!

Buy any assortment of twelve *Heartsong Presents* titles and save 25% off the already discounted price of $2.97 each!

*plus $3.00 shipping and handling per order and sales tax where applicable.
If outside the U.S. please call
740-922-7280 for shipping charges.

HEARTSONG PRESENTS TITLES AVAILABLE NOW:

(If ordering from this page, please remember to include it with the order form.)

Presents

HEARTSONG PRESENTS

If you love Christian romance…

$10.99

You'll love Heartsong Presents' inspiring and faith-filled romances by today's very best Christian authors. . .Wanda E. Brunstetter, Mary Connealy, Susan Page Davis, Cathy Marie Hake, and Joyce Livingston, to mention a few!

When you join Heartsong Presents, you'll enjoy four brand-new, mass market, 176-page books—two contemporary and two historical—that will build you up in your faith when you discover God's role in every relationship you read about!

Mass Market 176 Pages

Imagine. . .four new romances every four weeks—with men and women like you who long to meet the one God has chosen as the love of their lives…all for the low price of $10.99 postpaid.

To join, simply visit www.heartsong presents.com or complete the coupon below and mail it to the address provided.

YES! Sign me up for Heartsong!